A BETRAYAL

A Betrayal

and
Other Stories

Brian Biswas

Rogue Star Press
USA

"The Bridge" published in Penny Dreadful (December 1991), reprinted in Cafe Irreal (May 2006) and Tien Ve (June 2013)
"A Betrayal" published in Penny Dreadful (September 1999), reprinted in Cafe Irreal (February 2000) and the Irreal Anthology (November 2013)
"The Crystal" published in Penny Dreadful (July 2000)
"In the Garden" published in Cafe Irreal (February 2010)
"The Museum of North African Treasures" published in Lost Worlds (April 1993)
"This Old Man" published in Skive (June 2011)
"Solitary Confinement" published in Midnight Zoo (January 1992)
"Love in a High-Tech Age" published in Aoife's Kiss (June 2012)
"A Journey Through the Wormhole" published in Perihelion Science Fiction (June 2013)
"2038: A Mars Odyssey" published in Perihelion Science Fiction (September 2014)
"Barnegat Inn" published in Perihelion Science Fiction (January 2015)
"The Worms of Titan" published in Perihelion Science Fiction (June 2016)
"Puff" published in Perihelion Science Fiction (February 2017)

Cover art: www.kimdingwall.com
Author photo: Chris Florio

For information contact Rogue Star Press, an imprint of Lillicat Publishers. Books may be ordered through booksellers or by contacting Rogue Star Press at www.roguestarpress.com.

POD ISBN: 978-1-945646-41-6
EPUB ISBN: 978-1-945646-42-3
MOBI ISBN: 978-1-945646-43-0

To Elizabeth, of course!

Contents

THE BRIDGE

Night was beginning to fall as I started across the bridge; my journey had been unsuccessful, I wished now only to be home. My hands in my pockets, my lantern slung over my shoulder, I moved quickly ahead; I was long overdue, and my wife was surely worried: even from the start she'd expressed grave misgivings about my venture.

I was nearly halfway across when I thought I heard a cry rise up from the water below. I drew close to the edge and peered into the gathering darkness but saw nothing. Only the nighttime playing tricks—or so I thought; I shrugged and continued onward. But I had traveled no more than a few paces when the sound came again, unmistakable this time: a low, shivering moan. I crossed to the other side and, standing on tiptoe, I put my hands on the railing and peered into the water below. The moonbeams danced upon the effluent river, but I saw nothing portending imminent danger, only pieces of flotsam which bobbed restlessly about. I was turning to go when suddenly, unexpectedly, I saw what I wish now I never—never!—had seen: it was a body, floating upon the water, floating serenely upon the water, face downwards, it made no movement; it was not real—I repeat, it was not real—but to me it was real. And possessed by a flight of fancy I pulled off my clothes—a chance for success could not be dismissed!—and I dove into the water, my arms opened wide so as to snatch up this poor victim the water had claimed. "Hang on!" I cried as I dove through the air, but when I reached the spot from where the sounds had come, there was no one there, no one to save. At first, I felt a sense of relief, realizing no one had drowned, but that feeling, which can only be described as ludicrous in nature, gave way to one of abject horror, as I realized the full extent of my foolishness. Look what had happened to me!

The icy water caressed my face and I shivered uncontrollably; the river, which I estimated at some fifty yards wide, flowed sluggishly, as it had appeared to do from the shore, no deception there, and I was able to tread water with ease; the moon, shining over all, bathed me in a soft, pale luminescence; wavelets swirled around me, molding me, caressing me, and always the river's undercurrent tugged gently at my heels. I tried to swim to shore, but the waters, bewitched, held me fast. I could only float with the current which, though perceptible, seemed to carry me nowhere. At one point, I was certain I heard the laughing sounds of several travelers, drunk with their revelry, as they crossed the bridge, and I cried out repeatedly, my voice firm, urgent, but they paid me no heed.

Helpless and alone, unable even to struggle, I resigned myself to the inevitable: I was doomed. With only my lantern to guide me, I sank slowly into the depths.

A BETRAYAL

I had trekked nearly twenty miles that day to a village in an isolated region of our province. I am a doctor by profession; I had received a call from a family in the village of Tamborini. I had never heard of it, nor had my wife, though that was not unusual: our province is populated with small communities which are here one minute and gone the next. The caller had been an older woman, probably the victim's mother, and though I had never seen her before, I imagined her vividly as she stood before the phone: the receiver held tightly to her mouth, her left hand frantically brushing back her ash-blond hair, her lips tightly drawn, her skirt awry. In a frightened voice she told me that her daughter was sick: feverish and pale. She refused food and would not speak, but only stared at the ceiling, her eyes swollen and red. Might I come at once—this she implored me—before what they feared might happen happened and she was lost to them forever? I have always prided myself on doing whatever was called for to help another, and even though I had other patients to attend to that day, including one whose life at that moment hung in the balance, I tossed a few medical items into my knapsack, fueled my lantern, and set out at once, pronto, without even kissing my wife good-bye.

I must have been so eager to see my new patient that I paid no attention to the path before me, reflecting on the examination to come, the sinuous twists and turns of the country roads making no impression on my mind. In short, I quickly became lost and wandered about the countryside, nearly in a panic, futilely searching for the village of Tamborini. But it was not my day: the passersby whom I accosted had never heard of the place, except for one elderly gentleman who said the name sounded familiar, and might it be the headquarters of that traveling circus? It was beginning to look as though I'd been duped, as my wife had feared from the beginning. I never think anything through, she said, look at the way I was rushing about, throwing things into my knapsack, almost leaving without my lantern—and I certainly would have done so, if she had not stopped me!—and I was at the point of admitting defeat, and had even turned around to head back home, when, as if by magic, the village of Tamborini opened before me.

In the village square young girls and boys were playing and they gathered around me and stared. Impertinent youngsters! Hadn't they seen a doctor before? But then I realized that I hardly looked like a doctor: my clothes were tattered, my boots were muddied and—dear me!—I'd lost my knapsack; I remembered taking it off when I'd stopped to rest and I must have forgotten to put it back on when I resumed my journey. I've always needed to be constantly watched, as my wife is so fond of reminding me, and yet now my absent-mindedness was reaching alarming proportions! I asked the children where the family lived, and after a moment's hesitation, one of them pointed the place out to me. It stood near the outskirts of the village, near the banks of a wide river which flowed serenely by. I thanked them and started towards it, their snickers still resounding in my ears.

I'd imagined my patient's house to be like an imperial palace—don't ask me why, I'm prone to flights of fancy—but when I reached it, I saw that it was simply constructed, no more elaborate than an adobe hut actually, and also much smaller than I'd imagined. When I mounted the steps and let fall the wooden knocker, an elderly woman answered and ushered me inside. There on a couch next to a rickety wood stove I saw the daughter: dark brown hair, hazel eyes, shapely, demure, an aurora borealis of fragile beauty. The family was gathered around her in a half-circle, nearly on tiptoes, their arms interlocked. The girl was no more than seventeen and I knew at once what her problem was.

I opened my mouth to speak, intending first to console her, but she placed a finger to her lips, immobilizing me with a glance. "Say nothing," she whispered. "They will hear you."

"I am here to help you," I said, bringing my face close to hers, my lips to her cheek. She looked at me with innocent eyes, with longing, almost with love. She was quite pale, her eyes adrift, but she had no disease the medical establishment could cure.

"Please, keep silent," she repeated, "they must never know."

Know what, my child? I thought. *I know the general nature of your illness, that is true, but as to particulars, I have no idea.* I told her to speak plainly; no use trying to fool a doctor. The truth is always revealed in the end. She looked at me pleadingly, her eyes overflowing with the emotion of her youth. What I wanted was to take her into my arms, then and there, not out of love but a kind of compassion I felt for her. I could not do that, what with her family hovering about, but neither could I keep silent. I am a doctor. When a life is threatened, I will keep no secrets.

"Your daughter is in love," I said as the assembled gasped in disbelief, "It happens every day, but it is nothing to be afraid of. Do you know the boy?"

I would have expected them to be overjoyed, a girl—their child—was becoming a woman, but instead they seemed oppressed as if by a profound sadness.

"No, she is quite ill," her mother insisted. "At night she walks in her sleep and she moans."

"I do not doubt you," I replied. "Probably she is dreaming of her beloved."

"That cannot be," the mother continued, her voice growing weaker (for she herself did not really believe her words), "she is so young."

I never doubt the—often intense—feelings of a parent for a child, but in this case, they were mistaken: the girl was seventeen and she was in heat. I assumed she had denied a suitor her love, now regretted having done so; or perhaps it was she who had loved, but in secret, being too shy to reveal her desires. Again, I drew close to the daughter and again I examined her. And, again I reached the same conclusions. Yes, she did have a touch of fever, but it was nothing out of the ordinary, especially considering her lovesick condition. I wiped the perspiration from her forehead and bent over to give her a kiss, soft, unnoticed.

I rose and shook my head sadly. There was nothing they could do, I said; time alone would cure her.

The father protested—but feebly. "You must be mistaken. Perhaps, a second opinion . . ."

If they wished, but the diagnosis would be the same. A simple ailment requires a simple cure—and I could detect a pretty face as quickly as any man! All were silent, on hearing my words, and they gazed uncomprehendingly about. And then, without warning, another member of the family—was it a sister? or an aunt?—spoke up angrily and she arched her back in a gesture of supreme defiance.

"What kind of a fool doctor are you? Didn't you notice those red blotches on her cheeks and arms? And her fever—it's high enough to set the house on fire, but you didn't bother to check it. No, you noticed nothing. Too busy trying to peak inside her blouse. Dirty dog!"

The woman's accusations, completely unfounded, only aroused my ire. Imagine me, a respected doctor, my professionalism attacked! "Dear lady," I said, "I have no interest in the child, as lovely as she is, other than as a doctor's patient. Moreover, and I bristle even to have to say this, I am a happily married man; at my age the body of a young woman means little; the girl's flesh, though most succulent I am sure, does not arouse me."

The woman, overcome by the strength of my reply (had she expected me to break down and confess?), stared at the floor and said nothing further.

"Angelica," said the father after a long pause, "tell the doctor what truly ails you. Do not be afraid."

The girl said nothing but began to sob quietly into the pillow.

I sighed. "It happens to us all," I said. I knelt back down to the girl, to Angelica, and I brought my lips to her ear, so that only she could hear my words, "Good luck!" I whispered, and she broke into a radiant smile—she is so beautiful when she smiles—and picking up my lantern, which I'd left beside the door, I made my exit.

The journey home seemed to take forever, so muddled was my mind with thoughts of Angelica. No matter how much I might have wished otherwise, her prognosis did not look good. She was a doomed woman, of that I was certain, for her family would never admit her passions. It was clearly evident in their eyes—in their cold and icy stares, their belligerent voices—never would any of them admit to wrongdoing. The illusions we hold are often admirable, yet no more so than the lives ruined because of them. The love we feel but cannot convey is a stark reminder of our own limitations.

When I came out of my reverie and looked at the scenery about me, I realized I must have taken yet another wrong turn, for I hadn't the faintest idea where I was! And like Angelica I, too, felt betrayed. Betrayed by a family that had no respect for the medical establishment. Betrayed by country roads that didn't have the decency to take a weary traveler straight home to bed.

I sighed, pulled my overcoat tight, and pressed doggedly ahead. No doubt I was hundreds of miles from home by now, in some other province, some other land. *You've really done it to yourself this time*, I thought. *Your wife will never forgive you for this.* It's sad but it's true: one false step in this world and the Fates descend. And with that as my final thought I disappeared into the brooding darkness of the night.

THE CRYSTAL

My name is Odis Din, I am a lighthouse keeper, I am eighty-eight years old—nearly as old as the lighthouse I keep—but none of that is really important. What is important is my story. That it occurred late in my life is a blessing, for had it occurred when I was young, I would have spent the majority of my days in the most abject misery; that it had to happen at all, however, is a curse—for it has left me frightened and confused. It could have happened at any moment, though, and that is what truly frightens me.

I was born in Ere, a small town in Northern Europe, located on the edge of the great blue sea. The wise men of our town say that the sea stretches clear around the world, but I do not believe them. The world—as I know it—is flat, and how could the sea be so immense? I have not traveled very far out to sea, however, so I cannot say for certain. I am not one to prejudge the bizarre. Listen:

once I pulled a dying mermaid from the ocean; I nursed her to health and set her free in a cove not far from here. I found her again, several weeks later, washed up on the shore; I tried to touch her, but she drew away and returned to the sea. I never saw her again. And once I saw a majestic sailing ship, the pride of the King's fleet, an enormous vessel, swallowed up in calm waters—the sea simply opened, as the land does when the earth trembles, and the ship disappeared into the earth. I heard the cries of a hundred seamen—cries of surprise, of disbelief, and of anguish—as the sea closed over the ship. True stories both—though no one has ever believed me. When I was young, I made plans to build a boat and sail the length of the sea—if such a thing was possible. I said I would end up at one of the stars in the sky. My sister called me a foolish child. "Everyone knows the ocean empties into the mouth of a great dragon," she said. "If you embark on such a journey, you're sure to end up in the belly of the beast!" My sister died—one awful night she was swept away by the raging sea—and I vowed never to think such wild thoughts again. To believe that I, a mere mortal, could conquer infinity!

I lied a moment ago. I do not really know how old I am. I do know that I was born in the year 1860, or thereabouts. But what year it is now I have no idea. I no longer think about the years as they roll by. I stay secluded in the lighthouse—the lighthouse bequeathed to me by my father—I no longer venture into town. There I am known as a strange, old man. But why should that bother me, a man sick and tired of the world and its strange ways? The sooner man destroys himself the better. That is what I say.

One night not long ago I heard footsteps approaching the lighthouse and then knocks upon my door. Since I could not recall the last time I had had a visitor, I was somewhat alarmed. The door opened to reveal an elderly man, though not nearly as old as myself. He was wearing a gray overcoat. His face was weather-beaten, and his eyes were sad. He was also quite tall; indeed, I had never seen such a giant of a man.

"I need your help," he said. "I am from the province of Ambriilon and am traveling to Ungerston; but I fear that I have lost my way."

I invited him inside. He smiled and told me his name. "Clancy Barrows," he said. "Pleased to meet you." He had an awkward way of speaking.

"Yes," I said, after a moment's pause. "Ungerston is many miles to the south. I fear you have been traveling in the opposite direction." His sad eyes looked even sadder now and a low moan escaped his lips. "Do not worry," I continued. "You look hungry and I am about to have my evening meal. Will you join me at the table? Afterwards, I will give you directions to Ungerston. If you travel through the night, you will arrive before morning."

We ate a simple meal—muffins, eggs, and tea—and when we were finished he thanked me for my hospitality. A crash of thunder warned of a coming storm and I offered him a cot for the night. Now I am not the most sensitive of men, but even I could tell he was relieved.

I awoke several hours later. It was pitch black and the storm was raging. The lightning was magnificent—we are prone to brilliant displays of nature out here on the edge of the sea—and the thunder was deafening. I looked over towards my companion and I saw that his eyes were staring vacantly at the ceiling.

"Do not be afraid," I said. "The storm will pass. The storms are always violent on the edge of the sea."

"No, I have nothing to fear," he said. "The crystal will protect me."

I remember being puzzled at his words, but sleep overcame me, and I said nothing more.

When I awoke the next morning—it was half-past five; one hour before the dawn—the storm had subsided. My visitor was still asleep. I arose and, since it was quite cold, started up the fire.

When he awoke, and after we had eaten, I asked him what he had meant by his words of the night before. He smiled and pulled from his pocket a silver box. He opened the box and took out a tiny crystal ball. It gleamed faintly like highly-polished translucent glass.

"This will protect me," he said. "It protects whomever possesses it."

Intrigued by his words, I asked him to elaborate.

"The crystal contains light," he said. "It is the light of the beginning of time, of the world, of existence itself. Nothing is purer, and nothing can be purer, for it comes straight from the heart of our Lord. This crystal ball, which most men would not even notice, is mightier by far than even the King's armies!"

Now my curiosity was aroused to the extreme. Could this be the infamous philosopher's stone of which my father had often spoke? Or the black diamond of Karuka, which was rumored to lie deep within the heart of Africa? Many men had come to ruin in their search for that treasure. "Can this really be?" I said. "It sounds like such a wonderful gift."

"Ah, but it is true," was his reply. "This crystal protected me from the seven twisted horsemen of Narobe, who wrought havoc on the plains of Gall; it sheltered me from the women of Illad, who delight in a peculiar brand of torture; it cured me when I lay dying from the Black Death when all my friends had perished at my side."

And just then it occurred to me: how could such magic ever come into the arms of man? "You seem like such an ordinary person," I said. "Why were you chosen to receive such a treasure?"

"I was given this crystal ball by my father," he continued, "who received it from his, who received it from his, who stole it from a great king who is no more. All one needs do to summon the powers of the crystal is to speak the word."

He did so then—a word which filled me with awe; a word which I will never ever repeat—and suddenly the room was filled with a blinding white light, emanating from the very center of the globe.

I covered my eyes; the light was so bright I could make out only his face: radiant and pure, shining forth with a splendor all its own. I was silent. I would do nothing (and I am convinced to this day that I could have done nothing) to break the inner peace of that moment.

Some time later he passed his hand over the crystal ball and the light subsided. Then he put the crystal back into its silver box and he put the box into his pocket.

I expected him to leave but instead he sat down on the floor in the middle of the room and folded his arms across his chest, staring vacantly at the opposite wall. I asked what he was doing. He did not respond. I looked into his empty, gray eyes. I snapped my fingers. Nothing. *Well,* I thought, *there is nothing to be done. Leave him where he sits. He is a strange fellow. Eventually he will depart.*

I was preparing lunch when I heard a knock on the door. It was the village constable, a stout man with a serious face and coal-black eyes. He asked if he could come inside. I said no—not unless he had a warrant. He smiled. He told me a man had disappeared from the local hospital the day before and had been seen heading in this direction. Had I seen him? What did he look like? I asked. The constable described the man who had come to my door the previous evening.

"No," I said. "I haven't seen him."

The constable eyed me closely. I don't think he believed me. "Well," he said, "if he comes this way, let me know."

I assured him I would. He turned to go, and I added: "What was wrong with him, anyway?

The constable tapped the porch several times with the heel of his boot. He flicked his tongue across his thick lips. "He was under observation," he said.

"What do you mean?"

He paused. "Clancy tried to kill himself three days ago."

"Oh."

I shut the door and went back into the living room. I had to get this man out of my house. Whatever became of him, I didn't care. He was still there, sitting on the floor in a trance-like state. Like a child. I called his name. He did not acknowledge me.

"Wake up," I said, shaking him by the shoulders. "The day is half gone. If you don't leave now you won't make Ungerston by nightfall."

He stared at me with rheumy eyes. "The crystal . . ." was all he could say.

"You haven't a moment to lose."

He rose slowly to his full height. He rubbed his chin and scratched his nose. He seemed puzzled.

"Why didn't you turn me in?" he asked.

"I don't know."

"It would have been the simplest thing to do."

"Perhaps."

He looked around the room, studying its layout. Eventually, his eyes settled on the fireplace. The fire I'd started an hour before was going strong.

"Have you lived here long?"

He looked at me uneasily. I felt my palms beginning to sweat.

"Thirty-odd years," I said.

He said, "If I were to leave the crystal with you—only for a short while, mind you—would you promise to keep it safe?"

I was taken aback. I didn't know what to say.

"Well?"

"You hardly know me."

"Let's just say someone wants it and I think this is the last place he'd look."

Perhaps it was because I felt sorry for him, or maybe it was simply momentary weakness on my part, but I put aside my concerns and told him I would do so.

The man was gone for three days. On the first day I took the crystal out of its box. I set it on the kitchen table and examined it. The stone seemed ordinary now, like a schoolboy's marble. I passed my hand over it, as the man had done, but nothing happened. I put it away. Towards evening I wandered down the shore and gazed out at a blustery sea. The sky was pale-green, and the wind was blowing in from the south. The clouds lowered darkly.

Nothing happened the second day and I began to wonder if my fears had been unfounded. But the afternoon of the third day I once again heard a knock on the front door. I opened it—but saw no one. I went outside and looked around. Only shadows stealing across the yard in the waning light. That was odd. I had heard a noise. Perhaps the wind had blown a branch against the house? I looked up into a sky the color of lead. A dark sky that seemed to press down upon me. Dead black trees towered overhead, trembling in swirls of earthy wind. I went to the back, looked up and down the dirt road that ran past the lighthouse. It was empty. I shook my head. I went back inside—and received the shock of my life. There on the kitchen table, in plain view, was the silver box. The lid had been raised and the crystal was gone. Just then I heard a sound coming from my bedroom at the back of the house. I hurried down the hallway. The bedroom window was open, and the wind was blowing the curtains back and forth. I saw the outline of a man disappearing through the window. I saw his bird-of-prey hands. I sighed. I could only hope Clancy would never come back.

It was the very next day when the constable returned. Did I have any news to tell him? I shook my head, no. Did he? In fact, he did. Clancy had been found the previous evening, lying face down in the creek on the outskirts of town. The coroner estimated he had been dead no more than six hours, but, strangely, his face was already bloated, and the flesh was peeling from his bones. Needless to say, I was shocked. The constable eyed me closely. I think he may have suspected me of something. I told him it was a shame. He nodded. He just wanted me to know, he said. In case I'd been worried. I told him I appreciated his concern.

Another week went by, but I had no more visitors. My life was returning to normal and it was about time. The morning of the eighth day, however, I was awakened from a deep sleep by loud rapping at the front door. What now? Was the constable to arrest me for the murder of a man shrouded in mystery? I pulled myself out of bed, and cursing under my breath, went to the door and opened it. Clancy stood before me. He looked exhausted. His overcoat was muddied, and his clothes tattered. He was trembling and there was a strange expression in his insomniac eyes.

"Come in," I said.

He entered the house slowly, walking with a distinct limp. He sat down on the couch in the living room. He stared at the fireplace, as if mesmerized by the flames, but said nothing. There was a presentiment of death in the air.

I offered him a cup of coffee. He nodded. I went into the kitchen and brewed a pot. Then I went back into the living room. He took the proffered cup without a sound. His face looked soft and timid in the first rays of the dawn.

I stoked the fire and sipped my drink. "You're supposed to be dead," I said matter-of-factly. "Do you want to tell me what's going on?"

He sighed. He seemed gripped by an intense sadness. "It's quite simple," he said finally, and as he continued he steadily became more animated. "My father had many enemies. He was a good and decent man and good and decent men are often hated by those who envy them. Let me explain: when my grandfather died, he bequeathed to my father the crystal. Over the years, it brought my father great power—power my father's oldest son came to desire. My father knew of Seth's wishes, but he did not like—or trust—the child. I never learned the details, but apparently there had been several altercations between them. One day my father announced the crystal would be passed on to me instead. Seth never dared challenge my father while my father was living, but when he died, Seth grew bolder. He approached me and demanded I give him the crystal. My father was an old man when he passed away and, Seth said, was not in full possession of his faculties. He had certainly meant for the crystal to pass to his oldest son not his youngest. I was not amused. I knew what my father thought of Seth and I told him. The truth was not pleasant, and I did not mince words.

"Seth became angry. He called me names I cannot repeat. How dare I question the motives of an older brother, he said. He grew so upset the veins on his neck bulged. He continued yelling at me, his words growing louder and more vehement until I thought he was going to have a nervous breakdown. I told him to leave my sight. I never wanted to see him again. He stared at me helplessly and an ugly silence fell between us. Then he slunk away."

Clancy stopped. His face was red and puffy, and his hallucinatory eyes were bulging. I had never heard such poppycock. Without a doubt, the man was a lunatic. "I thought you were supposed to be in a sanitarium?" I said.

"I am not yet finished with my story," he said. His head tilted to the side and I detected the ghost of a smile. "The crystal has incredible power as I have told you. And it would not let Seth be. He pursued me far and wide, so strong was his desire to possess the crystal, until I sought refuge in a sanitorium near here. It was the one place he would never dare enter. He knew he was mad and that once inside he would never escape."

And then Clancy did what he never should have done. From beneath his overcoat he pulled out the crystal. It was glowing brightly, the light shining into my eyes like a beacon of truth. I gasped. For I saw in the crystal the world—and in the world the crystal—and I realized the true meaning of the wayward traveler's words.

"Where did you get that?" I stammered.

He laughed. "Seth stole it from you," he said. "But it did him no good. I was waiting for him by the creek and I killed him when he passed by. When the authorities came upon the body, they mistook him for me. And now I am free—and free of my brother forever." He paused, then added (somewhat smugly, I thought, since, after all, I had failed to protect his magic rock): "I simply wanted to thank you for helping me."

He turned to go.

Why is it that what we want we will never receive? And why is it that what we don't want we will always receive and always at the most unpropitious moment?

So, it was to be with me. Suddenly, and for some unknown reason, my mind was seized by the strangest idea: *I must have the crystal,* I thought. *Because it is so beautiful.* Imagine me, an old and dying man, overcome by an insatiable urge to possess! To this day I have not the slightest idea what overcame me. I offered him coins of gold and silver, which I had locked away in a strong box underneath my bed, everything I owned, but he refused. "Then I would no longer be safe," he said. "And besides, your earthly possessions mean nothing to me." He buttoned his coat and turned to go.

With one swift movement I pulled the poker from the fire and plunged it into his back. He fell dead without a sound. I stripped off his clothes, threw them in a ball into the corner, dragged him down to the edge of the sea, and with a groan, heaved his body in. The tide was going out and soon he was lost to view.

I returned to my room and unwrapped the clothes to reclaim my treasure. The crystal was gone. (Should I not have foreseen it?) At that very moment the sun broke over the horizon—I shall never forget that moment . . . a moment of revelation and despair—and the room was flooded with light. I thought that perhaps the crystal had fallen to the floor when I had stripped the man naked. I cursed God under my breath and, getting on my hands and knees, searched the room. I found nothing. Realizing that he must have hidden the ball in his mouth, or, perhaps, placed it in the palm of one of his enormous hands, I ran down to the sea and waited for his body to wash up on shore.

I know that he will eventually return, but I doubt that he will still possess the crystal ball. The sea is not one to easily give up her treasures.

Such is my story, and may God forgive me my sins.

TRAMP

Tramp may as well have always been there, trudging up the castle staircase. He could not recall a prior time. The staircase rose at a sharp angle up the castle tower, and though Tramp was in good shape, he grimaced from the exertion.

The tower was damp and musty. The lighting dim. Worn, wooden stairs creaked beneath his boots.

The first room, he thought. *On the left.*

Cobwebs clung to Tramp's face and neck, and cold air gnawed at his bones. He pulled his overcoat tight and clung to the metal railing, the hours dragging by as in the unreal time of dreams.

Just when Tramp was about to abandon all hope, the staircase began winding round in a dizzying spiral. That must mean he was nearing the top. If he had looked down, he would have noticed that the bottom of the staircase was no longer visible.

***

Though Tramp may have thought otherwise, he had not always been there, clinging to the staircase railing. There was a time that came before.

He no longer remembered how long it had been—months? years? centuries?—when thirty-year-old Tramp Dyer emerged from the forest that surrounded the castle, exhausted, his heavy backpack made heavier by the grueling journey he'd undergone. He'd traversed the ancient, rocky hills of the north and the fertile, green valleys of the central region, following the course of a winding river that ultimately led to the primeval forest which protected the castle from those who wished it harm.

Tramp was a carpenter from Zurau, a small town located a week's journey—on foot—from the castle. He was well-known for construction projects he'd undertaken in the province over the past decade and had been summoned to the castle to make repairs, the nature of which had not been specified. But when you were summoned to the castle, you obeyed.

When Tramp entered the front hall, he was met by a middle-aged woman with light-brown hair and laughing blue eyes. A bronze placard on her desk read: Amelia Page, Secretary. There was a silver bell on the desk, presumably to summon her should she be absent.

"Greetings!" A strong, forceful voice. "Can I help you?"

Tramp presented Amelia with the letter he'd received, setting forth the general request and terms of payment. Apparently, the authorities had neglected to inform her of his visit, for she looked puzzled. She glanced at the letter and remarked that it was not signed. She looked him up and down and then raised an eyebrow (in truth, Tramp looked like a tramp). She demanded to know his place of residence and asked to see his identification card. Her voice was stentorious and he stammered in confusion. Her suspicions aroused, she called headquarters to request authorization.

The voices on the other end of the line were a cacophony of odd buzzing sounds. A symphony of electric saws that filled the room with static.

"A Mr. Dyer here for his appointment," Amelia said. Static.

"As there is no entry in the appointment book—" Static.

"Shall I send him on his way?"

The static cleared. "Send him right up." Tramp had always assumed that the authorities were Olympian in nature with voices befitting mighty gods. Instead what he heard was thin, weak, and timid, like the squeaking of a mouse. And it seemed very far away.

Tramp interjected: "Where do I go? I see a tower ascending—"

"To the top floor, of course. The highest floor. Once there, it is the first room on your left."

He nodded.

"You'll need these," she added, handling him a torch and a box of matches. "In case the lights go out."

***

It occurred to Tramp that he'd met no one on the castle staircase. He found that odd. The authorities were known to work around the clock on matters of state; one had to make an appointment, weeks in advance, just to meet with them. There should have been a parade of people going up and down the staircase. Yet as far as Tramp could tell, he was the only person on the stairs.

As he ascended the staircase he saw a mural depicting the rise of civilization etched into the granite wall. From the dawn of man up to the modern era. And beyond. The mural went on and on, seemingly forever. Every panel carved in intricate detail. This must have taken years to assemble, Tramp thought as he admired the stately work.

The staircase ended at a three-foot-square opening in the floor of a room. No one was peering through. Tramp found that odd as well. After all, he had been summoned to the castle. There should have been someone to greet him on his arrival. With a grunt, he pulled himself up and inside the room.

The place was dark. Tramp could not find a light switch. He lit the torch and the darkness exploded in a flood of illumination. If this was castle headquarters, something dreadful had occurred. The walls were scorched as from a fire. Papers from an opened filing cabinet lay scattered on the bare wooden floor. Tramp saw overturned metal chairs. A tattered gray couch. A writing desk, the drawers of which were missing. A thick layer of dust covered everything. It was as if the place had been ransacked—and long ago. *Why didn't Amelia know about this?* he thought.

An ornate oval mirror on the opposite wall resembled the type of mirror one might find in a lavatory. Its wavy surface made the place look like a carnival fun house and he—Tramp—like some ghoulish entity. He noticed the impression his boots had made in the dusty floor; though he'd walked straight across the room, the tracks resembled a parabolic arc.

There was a bay window on one side of the room. Tramp had felt claustrophobic after his trek up the castle tower, and even more disoriented after his brief time in the room, and he welcomed the opportunity to look out over the castle grounds. It was pitch-dark. The forest would be out there, of course. He shuddered at the thought of the terrors of night that lay within.

It was then that Tramp noticed bright lights from a city in the distance. A pulsing metropolis that shown brilliantly in shades of blue, red, and gold. It must have lay far beyond the forest, for this area of the province was sparsely populated. And he found that surprising, for to be so visible at such a distance it would have been well-known. Yet he had never heard of such a place.

He gazed at the city awhile longer and then drew back into the room. Unfortunately, he wasn't paying attention; as he backed into the desk, he slipped and fell to the floor. With a cry, he landed on his back, finding himself facing the night sky.

How could he not have noticed before? The room had no ceiling! And now it was Tramp who was puzzled. Was it the nature of the room—its numerous oddities—which prevented him from noticing what was oddest of all? If not that, then perhaps the ceiling was retractable, and he tripped a switch when he fell. It seemed improbable, but one never knew. Especially in these times.

As Tramp gazed upon the darkness of night, he realized he had never seen the stars so pronounced, and he wondered just how far up the staircase he might have traveled. He even thought he heard the wind whipping overhead—or was that merely the exhalation of the heavens?

It turned out that Tramp had taken an awkward spill, and he found himself unable to rise. At least it hurt when he tried to do so, pain slowly spreading from the center of his back out to his arms and legs. All he could do was lie there and look out the maw of the room and up at the celestial sphere.

There was a dying flicker and the torch went out. As Tramp's eyes adjusted to the darkness, he saw more stars emerge, many quite brilliant. Soon the room was filled with starlight, rays reflecting off the mirror and onto the desk, imparting to it a luminescent glow he found oddly comforting.

When the pain in his back abated, he rose from the floor. He saw, in the radiant starlight, yellowed papers, the edges torn, strewn over the desk's surface. He picked one at random. An architect's drawing; the page numbered. A second page looked similar—and was also numbered. After putting the pages in order, Tramp saw that they were blueprints. They indicated that the room was not the top of the tower, but that additional floors capped by a gold-plated cupola had been planned.

Yet he could travel no farther; he had reached the end. What had happened to thwart the builders' efforts? Or had the tower been completed at one point and then destroyed? Perhaps that was the reason he had been summoned: to effect repairs. But what was their nature? Who would specify them? And was he really to work alone? Tramp had no intention of waiting around to find the answers.

He heard a rustling sound from above. He looked up and saw a hoard of bats, their long wings sweeping against the rafters. He shuddered.

He hurried back down the stairs, which seemed to take much less time than going up and emerged into an empty hall. He looked for the silver bell to summon the secretary, but it was not on her desk. The telephone she'd used to contact the authorities was gone as well. And Tramp noticed something else: his letter. It lay on Amelia's desk, exactly where she had first placed it. And it was covered with dust.

***

Outside it was early morning, the sun rising in a clear blue sky. Robins chirped merrily. A pair of squirrels frolicked in the dew that speckled the castle grounds.

Tramp spied a woman gazing at the slow-moving river which wound past the castle. She was probably in her early-twenties and was wearing a light-brown rustic dress with ruffled sleeves. Her long dark hair was loose and fell to her waist. The woman had a startled expression, as if she was contemplating an important matter and had reached an unexpected conclusion. He did not want to disturb her, but if she could throw light on his situation, it might benefit them both.

Tramp went up to the woman and, throwing open his arms, inquired about the castle. Who were the authorities? What had happened in the tower's headquarters? And where had Amelia gone? She looked at him vacantly, and Tramp found himself wondering if she even understood his words.

There was an opened book on the woman's lap, an oversized hardback. Tramp saw an engraved plate, finely drawn figures, scientific equations. When she noticed what he was doing, she closed the book and he read the title, the lettering embossed in mossy gold: *Mathematical Principles of Natural Philosophy*, by Sir Isaac Newton.

A puzzled look came over Tramp's face.

"It's what I'm reading," she said. "It's from long ago."

He nodded. She wasn't a deaf-mute, then; quite the opposite. And though he hadn't recognized her at first, as he looked at her more closely, he could have sworn that their paths had crossed.

"What's your name?" he asked.

"Spring," she replied. "Amelia is my mother, if that's what you're thinking. We used to live in the castle, but now it is forbidden."

"Why?"

She blushed. "I went to places that were prohibited."

To the tower's cupola, perhaps, Tramp thought. If indeed it had ever been completed. "I've been to the upper levels," he said. "There's not much there."

"It's been years since I set foot in the place," Spring said. "Though what you say doesn't surprise me. Even when I left, it was beginning to decay."

Tramp looked at the book. "You found that in the castle's tower, didn't you?" he said.

She smiled. "I took it when I left. I doubt it was ever missed."

He told her about the summons and the blueprints he had discovered. "I got the impression, though, that the place is deserted. Have the authorities moved on?"

"I wouldn't know," she said. "Though it does seem plausible."

He frowned. "If that's the case, why was I summoned? Or perhaps the summons was issued long ago and, for whatever reason, was only recently delivered."

"Yes," Spring said, "that's probably what happened. The courier service these days is in disarray."

Tramp turned around to take one last look at the castle and its majestic grounds. He heard the sighing of a gentle breeze. Puffy white cumulus clouds dotted the sky. A sky that had turned from blue to a mirrored silver.

Of course, he thought, as the revelation swept over him, *how could I have been so blind?*

Tramp was not certain, but he was reasonably certain, that he had stumbled upon a place of infinite dimension and possibility, the castle tower, which had proved so arduous to climb, reflecting upon its granite walls images not only of what was to come, but of what had come before.

And what of Spring? And Amelia? Or, rather, Spring alone. For if what Tramp suspected was true, Spring was not Amelia's daughter, but an image of her latter self, frozen in the mists of time.

He told Spring what he suspected, but she only looked at him strangely, seeming not to understand his words. (Or was it their implication which eluded her?)

"I mean," he said slowly, "have you considered the possibility that the castle is but a house of mirrors and that you and I, the castle grounds—even Zurau, where I am from—are all reflections, too?"

Was that a gleam of understanding in Spring's eyes? Tramp wasn't sure, but as if in response, or what he hoped might be a response, she bit her lower lip, ever so slightly. Then she turned back to her scientific treatise. And Tramp, realizing that his work there was done, went quietly on his way.

IN THE GARDEN

It was exactly one year to the day after I had completed my novel. It had been accepted for publication by the well-known publishing house J.J. and Sons and I was busy making the final editorial corrections. I had written a romantic novel in the style of the masters of the nineteenth-century, a novel full of passion and intrigue, sex and scandal, thunder and blood, and yet unlike that century's sometimes ponderous works, my novel was happily devoid of any greater meaning. My publishers assured me it was certain to be a runaway bestseller. I do not know why, but I was suddenly overcome by a desire to return to the willow grove where I had written the manuscript. (Perhaps it was because I wished to be alone, in what had proved to be the garden of my creativity, to gather my thoughts before embarking on this new—and undoubtedly hectic—phase of my life.) The willow grove was a serene and beautiful place, located on a hill overlooking a valley that was home to several family farms. I had spent my life on one of those farms but had relocated recently to the city of Essex to be closer to J.J. and Sons and to prepare for several book signings and a publicity tour which were planned.

I took a bus to the east side of Essex where the offices of the Central Railway line were located. There I purchased a ticket to the nearby town of Trinity. The willow grove was located a mile from Trinity on the outskirts of the town of Gallop Mills; it would be a pleasant twenty-minute walk.

Upon boarding the train, I went from coach to coach looking for a place to sit. The train was crowded, and I didn't find a seat until I reached the last coach. The passengers were a sorry lot, the very dregs of society. In the first coach, I saw several men who were drunk and two others who had passed out in the aisle, bottles of booze in their hands. In the second coach, I came upon a woman with blond hair and blue eyes who was openly flirting with two young men. She was wearing a yellow blouse with puffed sleeves and a red skirt that fell to her ankles. She was babbling like a little brook, but I couldn't understand a word she was saying. The air in a third coach was thick with cigarette smoke, so thick, in fact, that I could barely see the hand I held before me. Upon entering the fourth coach, I saw a middle-aged man with a rufous beard, his eyes blazing like red coals. A young girl was hovering over him. His shirt was unbuttoned, and she was running her long, thin fingers across his chest. I sighed in disgust. I found my own coach to be dirty and cold; rays of early morning sunlight streamed through the windows, illuminating seats that were littered with debris. When I sat down in my seat I nearly fell to the floor: the rickety wooden slats had rotted away. I rose, dusted myself off, and sat down in a second seat across the aisle. I found myself next to an elderly man with a thin, sallow face and small, myopic eyes. He was wearing a black suit, a newspaper folded neatly across his lap. I tried to strike up a conversation, but he scowled and looked away. *What's fine with you is fine with me*, I thought as I looked back out the window at the pretty countryside that was rolling by. I was upset and with good reason. The sooner I got out of here the better. I glanced at my watch. It was half-past eight. I would be at the willow grove by ten.

Every few miles the train stopped, and half a dozen passengers got off. I never saw anyone board the train. My late-night editing sessions must have finally caught up with me for soon I was fast asleep. The next thing I knew my eyes were fluttering open; I yawned and sat up. The coach was empty, a dappled sunlight fell upon the red carpet. I looked at my watch and was startled to see that it was five minutes past five in the afternoon! I hurried through each coach, looking for a steward to question, but I appeared to be the only person left aboard.

"When did we pass Trinity?" I asked the engineer when I reached the locomotive. I feared we'd traveled halfway across the province by now.

He looked at me, puzzled. "Trinity?" he replied, scratching his head. "There is no stop on this line for Trinity. In fact, I've never heard of the place."

I looked at him incredulously. "I was born near Trinity," I said. "A town called Gallup Mills. I know it's on this line. I've made the trip many times before. It's a pleasant forty-five-minute run. And besides, only this morning I purchased a ticket to Trinity—aboard this train." I held out my ticket for him to see.

He looked at it and laughed. "This ticket is for the town of Tyron. The ticket taker misunderstood. But it doesn't matter: we stopped at Tyron several hours ago."

I didn't know whether to believe the engineer or not. I knew Trinity existed; I had spent my entire life nearby! But on the other hand, he was correct: we should have reached it a long time ago.

My strange day was only to grow stranger. I looked out the window and saw that we were approaching another town. I saw cars and a bus. Pedestrians. A girl on a bicycle. The train whistle blew, and we pulled slowly into the station. The engineer spoke:

"Sir, this is the town of Bynum; it is the end of the line. Regardless of what you think your ticket says, you must get off now."

I returned to my seat—giving the engineer a look of annoyance as I did so—picked up my carry-on bag and got off the train, emerging onto a vacant platform. It was half past five. The station had closed for the day. I glanced up at a sky that was gray and sad.

When I looked down, I saw a most unusual scene. There was a man in a horse drawn carriage adjacent to the platform. He was an elderly man, with dark-brown hair, rheumy eyes, an ugly scar across his neck. He was wearing a dark jacket with brass buttons and a white necktie. Black leather boots. He must have seen me looking in his direction for he said, "Where are you headed?"

"Gallop Mills," I said, fully expecting him to burst out laughing, but he replied simply:

"Get in."

He snapped a whip and his steed roared off. We traveled with lightning speed, the coach sashaying from side to side. I had to hold onto the sides to keep myself in. I expected us to backtrack, for the train had overshot my destination by many miles, but we headed further into the hinterland. I called out to the driver in dismay. He turned in my direction, his left hand cupped to his ear. "What was that?" he cried. "What did you say?" He was grinning fiercely, and his eyes darted like lightning. I slumped back into my seat.

I was amazed then, when, perhaps fifteen minutes later, the sign to Gallup Mills came into view. Small single-family houses on the outskirts of town. An old farmhouse. A wheat field. My heart was filled with joy. Moments later we were entering the downtown area; the driver pulled up to the red bricks of Central Square. I exited the coach and brushed myself off, checking myself over as I did so. I was none the worse for wear.

"How much?" I asked, pulling out my wallet. But when I looked back up he was nowhere to be seen. No—there he was, off in the distance. I watched the coach as it lurched away down the dusty road, shuddered at the sight of the coachmen's ghoulish form in the tenebrous light.

I left the square and turned onto the town's main street. Ten minutes later I was on the outskirts of town, looking out over a valley. I saw pretty, white houses that dotted the landscape, an enormous grove of orange trees, a pasture in which cows and horses grazed. I looked to my left and saw that I was at the base of a hill. It was at that moment that my first revelation of the day occurred. The day's events had left me disoriented. Only now did I realize that this was the valley I had been seeking, this was the valley I knew so well. I was filled with a sense of peace and of calm.

Breathless with excitement, my heart thumping like a piston, I ran up the hill. I was returning to a place of discovery, a place that had altered the course of my life and was about to alter it once more and overcome by a sense of wonder and of awe, I reached the top of the hill, crossed the edge of the willow grove, and there in the center of the grove I came upon a magnificent garden. I saw flora that I knew so well: chrysanthemum, honeysuckle, periwinkles, poppies, and daffodils. But also, flowers and vegetation I had never seen before: purple roses and phosphorescent orange moss, blue daisies and lime-green ferns.

This was not as I had remembered it. The willow trees that bordered the garden were the same—there was the tree under which I had composed my masterpiece—but the garden itself had been transformed from a simple place to one of fiery beauty. I walked through the garden—the grass beneath my feet lush and inviting—gazing in wonder at the scene around me, drowning myself in the intoxicating aromas of a thousand roses, of orange azaleas, flowering peppermint trees, pink mimosas. And it was then that I felt myself losing consciousness. I tried to hang onto this strange reality in which I found myself, but I was unsuccessful and moments later I was overcome with a deep sleep.

I had a dream: I was floating in space, looking out over the heavens. I watched as a comet moved slowly by. Unexpectedly, it turned and started towards me. I was swept up in the tail of the comet; I dodged particles of dirt and ice, felt gravity's gentle pull. I traveled slowly through the universe. I was not afraid. I saw other worlds go past: galaxies, nebulae, and enormous clouds of floating dust. Suddenly, all of it vanished and I was alone in a black void. Feelings of loneliness and despair swept over me, like waves over a drowning man. I was lost in a vacuum, there was nothing to steer by, and I had no place to come to rest. I looked out over the void and I saw that it was turning blood-red. And then I realized it was not the universe but the edge of creation I was seeing and that I was hurtling through space and time, like an arrow towards its fiery destination. When I passed through that end of time (which was also a beginning) I found myself in a whirlpool of color and light and from the depths of that whirlpool rose a vision and in that vision a series of words appeared before me (written in blood in that kaleidoscope which was my dream), words which by themselves were meaningless but when read together tantalized me with a significance I struggled to grasp.

The next thing I knew I was wakening to a new day; the sun was coming up over the valley. I yawned and sat up. The garden was quiet and peaceful, the air pure and still. I realized, then, that I would never return to Essex; I wished to spend the rest of my life here, amongst the people and places that I loved. J.J. and Sons would have to promote my book without me. And that was fine. I did not care about it anymore.

I looked out over the valley of my youth and sighed realizing I had reached the end of my journey.

There is nothing more to tell.

The world is wonderful and full of magic. He who does not believe it so is dead.

THE MUSEUM OF NORTH AFRICAN TREASURES

O nce there was a man named Robert Walsh. He was an assistant professor in the archaeology department at the University of Paris. Robert was in his mid-thirties, tall, dark, slenderly built. He was not handsome in the European sense of the word, but certainly was not unattractive and, like all professors who want to make a name for themselves, was quite energetic. But nothing Robert did to try and improve his position at the University seemed to work: He submitted archaeological proposals to prestigious journals. None were accepted. He applied for research grants (including the prestigious Young Investigator's Award) but was always turned down. Eventually, Robert decided his talents lay not in research but in management and he applied for a managerial position within the university (Chairman of the Physics Department, to be exact, this even though he had no formal training in the field). His application was not taken seriously by the search committee and Robert found himself the butt of jokes from his colleagues.

One day the following advertisement, in a local Parisian newspaper, caught Robert's eye:

ATTENTION ACADEMICIANS!

The Museum of North African Treasures, a provincial museum located in the middle of the Sahara Desert and one with an outstanding reputation, offers scholars beautiful surroundings, serenity, and support while they go about their studies. The Museum offers private study space for six scholars per month, with residencies ranging from two weeks to six months. No reasonable proposal refused. For more information write to MNAT, Sahara Desert, Central Provinces, N.A.

It's worth a try, thought Robert and without a moment's delay he wrote up a proposal and sent it off to MNAT. Several days later he received a letter stating that a place for him had been reserved! Robert was quite excited. Here was the chance he had been waiting for.

In a talk to the university's sabbatical committee (they also had to give their approval), Robert set forth his theory that in ancient times North Africa was home to a race of superior women; they were not only exceedingly beautiful, but also immensely powerful and had controlled the region for several centuries. He hoped to find evidence of such a civilization in the maps of the period. Much to Robert's surprise his talk was well received, and his proposal was accepted. (In truth, the sabbatical committee welcomed an opportunity to send Robert elsewhere, although they did not tell Robert that.)

***

Now it was the morning after Robert's arrival at the museum and he was standing on the museum balcony with the curator at his side. The balcony overlooked a large courtyard which was immaculately kept and contained a majestic spiral walkway that wound through several flower gardens. The horseshoe-shaped museum was curved on both sides, the north and south wings encircling the courtyard, except for the iron gate at the courtyard's base through which Robert had entered. Robert, however, was not interested in the layout of the place. He was staring in disbelief at a gigantic bird that was strutting about the courtyard, the likes of which he had never seen.

"It was truly a remarkable find," the curator said, and he indicated with a sweep of his hand the giant bird in the courtyard below. The curator was a small middle-aged man, balding, with an elongated droopy face and tiny black eyes. He wore brown trousers and a faded, plaid shirt, unbuttoned at the collar. He was staring at the bird with a look of admiration usually reserved for one's own child. The curator stood transfixed for a long time and then, with a sigh, he turned to face Robert. "Your room is simply furnished, but will prove adequate, I am sure," he said as he took Robert inside. The museum contained several small apartments set aside for visiting scholars and foreign dignitaries. Robert had expected to be put up at a local hotel and he said as much, but the curator simply shrugged. "Out here amongst the nomads of the desert," he said, "there is no other place to stay." Robert found his room to be sparse, as the curator had stated: a bed, a bureau, a writing desk. Nothing more. He put his bags next to the desk and went into the adjoining bathroom to wash up before dinner. His daylong bus ride across the Sahara had left him exhausted.

Robert and the curator dined alone that evening. Robert wondered where the other scholars were, and he was about to ask, when he thought better of it: he had no desire to appear impertinent; perhaps the museum had fallen upon hard times? As they ate, Robert tried to discuss the ancient art of map making. But his host wanted to talk only about the bird. He had captured it, he said, in the jungles of Central Africa; it was one of the last of its kind: a living monument to a vanishing breed. The curator was quite explicit as he told Robert all about the bird's anatomy, its eating habits, its behavioral aspects, how it reproduced. This last characteristic was particularly interesting: it seems the birds could not reproduce in the natural way, that is, by sexual intercourse. Rather they were so shy the female laid her eggs under a bush, then ran off and hid, as though the deed was too disgusting even for her to watch. The male, passing through and apparently disinterested, but actually peeking under each bush he encountered, upon discovering an egg, fertilized it quickly—and hurried off, as if in shame. Apparently, the egg was never touched or even seen by the parents again and the young bird had to fend for itself from the moment it was born.

"And it is rumored," the curator continued, "that the female pursues the male, kills him, and eats the body as a sadistic end to this strange ritual."

Robert gasped, and the curator added quickly:

"But it is only a rumor—it has never been confirmed."

Robert told the curator he would love to get a closer look at the bird the next morning. The curator grew pale: "No, no, no!" he cried. "You are here for a cartographic investigation, not to examine my pets!" He looked at Robert coldly and Robert felt himself shudder. He had the feeling the curator was hiding something, but he did not want to offend his host by inquiring further. The curator forced a smile and said: "I'm sorry. I didn't mean to frighten you. You see, I'm simply concerned for your safety. That bird is a creature of the desert; it is wild and untamed. And it has been known to bite!"

Just at that moment a young woman entered. The curator had mentioned he had one child, a girl of seventeen and very lovely, too, a remark with which Robert, upon seeing the girl, instantly agreed. "This is my daughter, Tamba," said the curator and he pointed towards the girl. Luckily for Robert, the curator had turned the lights low (this to provide a suitable atmosphere for his bird tale) and Tamba was not clearly discernible. Even so, he could tell that she was pretty: her eyes soft, her body curvaceous. I say Robert was lucky because if, at that moment, he had seen the full extent of Tamba's beauty, he would have been unable to control himself. And with who knows what consequences!

After the meal, the curator escorted Robert to the museum library. It was a small room, the oak walls lined with books, a map case in one corner. "This is what you came for," said the curator, motioning Robert towards the map case.

Robert opened the top drawer and pulled out several maps. He was examining them casually—they were maps of ancient China and were not particularly interesting—when he realized someone else had entered the room. He looked up: it was Tamba. "Hello," he said—and then he gasped: such beauty he had never seen!

"Pleased to make your acquaintance," she replied, but she did not look at him directly.

She's shy! thought Robert; then he said, "You are as lovely as your father claimed," and as he looked at her closely he saw that her beauty was many times what the curator had suggested. For every man there is a woman who will inflame him with passion (and for some men, many such women), and now Robert found himself faced with just such a woman. Tamba stood before him, wearing a long dark skirt and light-blue blouse, her long black hair pulled back over her shoulders. Her eyes were so pale they looked almost pink (Robert had never seen anything like them), her complexion was clear as morning dew. Her face had an empty expression, as if her thoughts were somewhere else.

Actually, Tamba was quite interested in Robert (for reasons that had nothing to do with romance). But Robert did not realize her true intentions and he continued for a long time blushing like a schoolboy. *She is the most beautiful woman since the beginning of time*, he thought. When Robert realized he was gaping at Tamba, he turned back to his work. When he looked up later, she was gone.

The next day Robert was up bright and early. After a breakfast of eggs and toast he hurried to the map room to begin his studies. Secretly, Robert was hoping Tamba would be there to greet him, that they would get to know each other better, perhaps go for a stroll on the museum grounds. But she was nowhere to be seen.

Nine o'clock, ten o'clock. Still no sign of Tamba. At noon the curator entered the room with a tray containing Robert's lunch. He asked Robert how the morning had gone. "Very promising!" said Robert. "I think my investigations will soon bear interesting results!" The curator smiled—an eerie smile that only unnerved Robert—then he said, "I trust that they will." He turned abruptly and left the room.

By mid-afternoon there was still no sign of Tamba. Robert decided to take a walk through the museum hallways. Perhaps he would find her in another part of the museum.

But in the hallways, he saw no one. In fact, not in the lobby, nor the library, nor any of the living quarters or study areas did he come upon a soul. Robert returned to his room and looked out through the open window at the museum grounds. Maybe Tamba was taking a walk with her father in the courtyard? There he saw, to his amazement, the curator with a bucket in one hand and a scrubbing brush in the other. He was giving the bird a bath! Now, that seemed ludicrous enough, but what was even stranger: the curator was talking lovingly to the bird as he bathed it; the words carried right up to Robert's window.

"How does that feel, my pet? Yes, you're so clean now. You'll sleep easier . . . no more dirt; you're always so dirty, my pet, rolling in the dirt like a pig—what did you say?" —the bird had squawked— "The new scholar? Yes, an interesting man. Rather abstruse, but—"—another squawk—"You want to eat him? Of course, you do, my pet; but you promised after the last one that there would be no more—"

At this point Robert could not suppress a cry: "What in the world—" he began, then caught himself. It was too late: the curator had turned around and was looking up at Robert's window. Robert drew back from the window and rushed from the room. His mind was more confused than ever: Had the curator seen him? And if so what had he thought, knowing Robert had heard his words?

As luck would have it, Robert nearly ran over Tamba, who was coming down the hall from the opposite direction.

"Excuse me, sir," Tamba said as she picked herself up and brushed the dust from her skirt. Upon recognizing Robert, she smiled. Then she said, "Professor Walsh—is something wrong? You look like you've had a dreadful fright!"

Robert told her of the strange scene he had just witnessed.

"There is no reason to be alarmed," Tamba said. "My father is eccentric, that's all. And he's always talking to that crazy bird."

Robert smiled. "Yes," he said. "I knew there was an explanation." He mumbled an apology for running into Tamba, then started on his way again, but before he realized what was happening Tamba had thrown her arms around him and begun kissing him about the face and neck, her fingers raking his back. Robert found himself in the awkward position of having to rebuff her advances (he did not want to jeopardize his stay in the museum by being discovered in a compromising position with the curator's daughter). He tried to push Tamba away, but she clung tightly to him.

"Tamba, please!" Robert cried.

Tamba kissed Robert on the mouth and said, "Professor Walsh! I want you!"

"But, Tamba—"

Just then Robert heard footsteps coming down the hall. He was still trying to free himself from the clutches of the girl when from out of the shadows appeared the curator, livid with anger.

"Professor Walsh!" he cried. "What are you doing with my daughter! Sir how dare you be so bold!"

Robert apologized, insisting he had no idea what had come over him. (He did not wish to implicate Tamba in any way.)

"And it had better be the last time!" cried the curator. He took Tamba by the arm and escorted her down the hall. He gripped her firmly by the neck, but even so, Tamba managed to turn half around and blow a kiss towards Robert, yet another sign of her love for him (as if Robert needed any more convincing!). Robert returned to the map room where he spent the remainder of the day alone, thinking only of Tamba and what a future with her might bring.

Robert did not see Tamba for several days. But her presence he always felt. Dark, mysterious, it filled the room where he studied, the halls where he walked, the bed in which he slept. By now he realized he was hopelessly in love with her; she ruled his mind—to put it bluntly—and he desired nothing but to make love to her. But she had vanished—and he had never even told her of his love! One night she came to him in a dream. He was in another realm; he had never known such happiness. *I will never pursue another woman*, he thought. But when he awoke (drenched in sweat) and realized it was an illusion, he was more miserable than ever. *If only she will come back to me*, he thought. *But where has she gone?* Robert was losing his sanity. She was everything he had ever dreamed of in a woman. But he could not have her.

The next morning Robert asked the curator what had happened to his daughter. "Tamba goes where Tamba wishes!" the curator snapped, evidently still upset over the events that had occurred that one afternoon. But then he seemed to calm down: he told Robert that Tamba had gone on a trip (but he did not know where), with a girl friend (but he did not know who). The curator's manner struck Robert as odd—and the way he was screwing up his eyes did nothing to alleviate Robert's suspicions.

That afternoon Robert went to the map room to study a map of thirteenth century Iquanoland (he was hoping that work might help him forget his troubles). But no sooner had he set his eyes to the paper when his attention was caught by peculiar scrawls in the margin of the parchment. They were faint and nearly imperceptible. But they were also undeniable. He picked up a magnifying glass to examine them more closely.

This is what he read:

"From the moment I met you, darling, I knew we were destined for each other's arms. My father is an evil man and he does not understand my needs, my wants—my craving for love. You may think that is bad enough, but what is worse: he has forbidden me to see you, to touch you, to even speak to you! And I am withering away—my lusting body drying up without your love. Still, forever I will remain your dearest love. Tamba."

The text wound round the margins of the map; the writing was swift and hurried, evidently Tamba had stolen into the room under fear of discovery and had only a few moments to leave her message, her message of love to Robert.

The next several days brought more of the same: more notes of burning love, this followed by notes of anguish and despair: the curator was keeping Tamba prisoner, in isolation and with little care. Soon the storm that rocked Robert's mind reached a feverish pitch. At dinner one night, Robert's host was telling him more stories about his bird, but Robert could stand the strain no longer. He rose up and banged his fist on the table. "Your daughter!" he cried, and the strength of his voice surprised even himself, "Where is she!" The curator looked at Robert in alarm—the fire in Robert's eyes was so intense it must have scorched the curator's soul—but he said nothing. And in his wild mania Robert grabbed his dinner knife and plunged it into the curator's chest. A dozen times he did so! Robert was so out of his mind that he dragged the curator's body through the museum and threw it into the courtyard. He made no attempt to conceal it. "Let that be your dinner," he said to the bird, which had eyed him warily the entire time.

That night Robert hardly slept, not because of the murder he had committed, but because Tamba was not at his side. The next morning the hallways echoed with the sound of his footsteps as he raced through the museum, throwing opens doors in a wild search for Tamba. Nowhere did he find her. Robert was in such a state of despair he did not think he would last the day.

Later that afternoon he returned to the map room, hoping to discover yet another message from his love. His face was pale, his eyes sunk deep in their sockets. And you can imagine the joy he felt when, written in the margins of a map he held before him—a map of ancient Greece which he had examined countless times—he saw a final note from Tamba. She had escaped the clutches of her father, she wrote, and was hiding in the depths of the museum. She urged Robert to meet her in the courtyard at dawn, there to be together at last! Robert drank up the words like an elixir: the moment he had longed for was soon to be.

Unfortunately for Robert things were not as simple as they appeared. Tamba was not being held prisoner in the museum's lower levels; she was in her own bedroom, in her own bed, weeping tears of grief for she had seen her father's body lying in the courtyard. The man who had found her half-starved in a village in Central Africa, abandoned by her parents (of her natural parents Tamba had no recollection; she dreamed once that she had eaten them, but of course that was mere fancy), who had nursed her back to health (and if he tolerated her one strange habit, well, some people love in the oddest ways), who had literally become her father—this wonderful man was dead. Killed by Robert while in an uncontrollable rage, a member of the grounds crew told her; he had seen the frightening episode with his own eyes.

Early the next morning Robert stole into the courtyard. The sun was beginning to rise, and reflecting off the date palms, it cast the shadows of dragons. But Tamba was nowhere to be seen. Robert was puzzled. Tamba's directions had been specific: "Under the silvery date palm, there we shall consummate our love." The words had filled Robert with such excitement he had been unable to sleep the night, his mind filling with images of Tamba and her intoxicating beauty. His heart throbbed at the thought of the ecstasy he would feel when he held her in his arms. And when she learned that her father—the tormentor of her soul—was gone forever from the Earth—then her heart would swell with joy and the lovemaking which would surely ensue would delight even the mighty gods above! But, where was she? The courtyard gates were open and outside Robert saw the desert, shimmering with heat. The sky was an unusual shade of blue: bright and metallic, such as Robert had never seen before.

"Robert."

He turned around and there he saw her: his beloved Tamba, standing next to a date palm tree. She was wearing a beautiful light-blue dress, which she removed as she started towards him.

"Robert."

He fell into her arms, weeping uncontrollably, like a man who is starved for love. Tamba looked at him with eyes that were filled with longing. She stroked his cheeks, caressed his face (her nails were quite long, and Robert cried out in pain when, at one point, she began scratching his neck). Then they fell to the ground, locked in that eternal embrace which is love.

When Robert awoke the sun was directly overhead. He reached over to touch Tamba, but his hand felt only the stones of the courtyard. He sat up and looked around. Where had she gone? The courtyard itself was nearly deserted. The only living creature in sight—other than himself—was that bird, now fast asleep, not ten feet from him. Tamba must have gone to prepare their lunch, Robert thought; and what a glorious feast it would be: leg of lamb, imported cheese, exotic fruits, and wine! While Robert was thinking about the coming meal, he continued staring at the bird. Robert had never been so close to it before and he saw now that the bird's skin was pearly white; it looked velvety smooth, like the flesh of a new born babe. Robert was suddenly overcome by the oddest sensation: he felt an intense desire to *touch* its skin. Robert recalled the curator's words of warning but dismissed them with contempt: The old man was senile, he thought. If the bird bit him he must have deserved it. Robert approached the bird on tiptoe, his arms outstretched, and lightly, ever so lightly, reached out and touched a small patch of skin underneath its belly. The bird opened one eye, slowly, and then the other. Rays of early morning sunshine struck its pupils and Robert gasped in horror as he saw the eerie *pink* eyes of the beast; they bore into his body like gimlets, rooting him to the earth. It was then Robert realized the inconceivable: this was no avian mutant, but Tamba herself who stood before him!

"Please, no!" Robert cried, and he drew back in horror.

Tamba laughed.

"Once it was within your power to leave here," she said, as she extended her talons, "but now it is too late."

Robert's body flooded with pain as Tamba dealt him the final blow. And as Robert fell to the earth he realized, in that fleeting moment before his death, that his punishment, though it at first appeared harsh, had really been most merciful.

THIS OLD MAN

Grace passed through the front doors of the Charlemagne Public Library on a sunny Tuesday afternoon, a stack of books under her left arm, a red silk rose affixed to her chiffon blouse, her favorite bright blue sunbonnet upon her head. It was a hot summer day. She passed the Fountain of Saint Gabriel a block from the library across the street from the police station and she admired as she always did the spray that shot skyward and reflected all the colors of the rainbow. Behind the police station loomed Charlemagne High, where she would be entering tenth grade that fall. She turned into a narrow alley that curved like a serpent and eventually ended at a side street that would take her back home, when she saw not ten feet from her in the dappled afternoon sunlight an old man slumbering under a pine tree. His clothes were tattered, and his feet were bare and callused, and a light-blue handkerchief protruded from his shirt pocket and fluttered in the humid breeze that seemed to come from all around. Grace did not know whether to return to the library and take the long way home—her parents had warned her to stay away from vagrants—but instead she continued towards this strange apparition, drawn ahead by something she did not understand. When she reached him, she stopped, and she stared into his ashen face as wrinkled as a prune, his stark-white hair, what might have been the remains of a scar on his neck, his arms and legs as thin as match sticks. And suddenly it occurred to her that he might be dead—he was clearly a very old man and the town was in the grip of a heat wave and maybe he had simply chosen this moment and this place to die—but just then his eyelids fluttered open and she gasped. The man looked at her with his two gray eyes that were filled with solitude and he uttered a single word: "Water."

Grace ran back down the alley, past the police station, almost running into an officer who was coming down the front walk and whose cry she ignored, and she stopped in front of the Fountain of Saint Gabriel where she held her bonnet open with both hands and filled it until the water overflowed and ran down her fingers. It was icy cold—cold enough to revive the thirstiest of strangers. A blast of hot air swept across her face and she looked up into an aqua sky and saw the sun beating down without mercy. God, she had never known it to be so hot! She resisted the urge to drink from the fountain and she hurried back down the street and into the dusty alley, past scaly lizards who stared at her with gargoyle eyes. Her heart was slamming in her chest.

"Drink this," she said, pouring the water into the stranger's gaping mouth. He seemed almost to choke on the life-giving liquid and his arms, which up until then had faithfully held him up like two pillars of steel, collapsed under his weight and he fell back with a sigh and lay still. He must have been very handsome in his youth, Grace thought as she admired his sparrow hands and his long, slender arms. A princely man who made the ladies sigh. But it was not until she touched his mottled skin and found that it was as soft as honey that she realized here was a man with the power to confuse time.

Just then she heard the cries of children coming down the alley. She turned and saw Sue and Sally and Peter and little Jimmy and there was not a grown-up among them thank God and they were laughing and singing and Grace did not know what to do for they were about to come face-to-face with a maddening wind. She looked at the library which could still be seen in the distance, at the ivy that preyed upon the solemn red bricks, the window on the third floor before which she had spent numerous afternoons daydreaming of knights and dragons, but not this day, not this hour, not this time.

"Oh, look at that," one of the children said when they drew near and saw in the dappled light an old man half-hidden in a pile of rotting leaves. "A dead man."

And he really did look dead with his tongue lolling in his mouth, his eyes wide-open and staring into space, his muscles gripped in the tremors of rigor mortis. Yet Grace knew he was not dead but dying and she talked the children into dragging the man to their clubhouse in the woods that ran alongside the alley where he could pass away in peace.

It was during dinner that evening that Grace's father announced that there had been an escape from Central Prison in the nearby town of Ridgeville and that the convict, a Mr. Peter Sturdivant, age thirty-three, was still at large. According to the police report, Sturdivant could be identified by a two-inch scar across his neck. He had been wounded by a young officer who shot at him with wild abandon, a bullet that struck his right thigh and would only make him more dangerous. "A convicted murderer," Mr. Lewis added. "He'll be thirsty for blood."

As it turned out, the old man did not pass away; in fact, under Grace's watchful eye, he slowly began to recover. She waited on him hand and foot, bringing him food she snuck out of the kitchen: apples and oranges, fruit juice, potato soup, egg salad sandwiches, leftover roast beef stew; towels soaked in ice water to help him stay cool during the late afternoons when the air in the clubhouse became unbearable and it was so hot that even the lizards in the woods were overcome with despair; two pairs of her father's pajamas one of which he wrapped around his head so tightly that he looked like a sultan and she could not help but laugh; and the evening paper which she bought with her own money from the corner drugstore and which was filled with stories about the search for the escaped prisoner which it seems was going nowhere. The children came by after the sun had gone down and the air had become tolerable once more and they all played games, tiddlywinks and crazy eights and Chinese checkers and when the stars came out Grace told ghost stories and clapped her hands, and everyone trembled with fear. For his part the old man chuckled at his good fortune, but he never said a word.

It was not until another week had passed that the old man began to come out of his shell. It started with an inconsequential gesture. Grace had left her home at eight A.M. as usual, walking quickly under an ashen sky, past the flower garden in her back yard, where she smelled rose blossoms and honeysuckle, saw butterflies with iridescent wings, heard songbirds gaily chirping. In the alley a striped lizard crossed her path and she stepped aside to avoid it, and then she entered the woods at the place where she always entered, pushing through the crenelated myrtles and stepping in as if entering another world. She held in her hands a silver tray containing the old man's breakfast and when she set the tray on the dusty wooden floor beside him his hand brushed against her arm. He had not meant to do so, he knew she was easily startled, he would never have wished to frighten her. But she was frightened, and she drew her arm away. His eyes slid over her, but he said nothing. "I'm sorry," she said, and she realized her adolescent words sounded strange as soon as they left her mouth but there was nothing else she could say, and she left him then, opening the clubhouse door and disappearing into the woods from where she had come.

That night Grace was visited by fiery dreams. She saw the old man in a dimly-lit morgue, lying naked on a cold steel slab, and she looked down on him and he looked like a puppet lying there with his papier-mâché nose and his thin lips and his eyes that seemed to have fled his face and the scar across his neck like a bold tattoo and he was stone cold and there was not a thing she could do. A curtain of sleep fell upon her then and when she awoke the next morning she resolved never to be alone with the old man again.

It was a Saturday morning in the middle of August, a time filled with trepidation—for the infamous prisoner was still at large, rumored to be both desperate and sick—when the old man finally spoke. The children were gathered around him as they were every Saturday morning and little Jimmy was teasing him about the stubbly gray beard that adorned his face. The old man had been living in the clubhouse nearly four weeks by this time and had been forced to endure all sorts of childish manipulations. He had been fed like a baby with a silver spoon and dressed in the morning like a toy soldier or a priest or a handsome prince and paraded around the woods like a trophy, except that there was no one to see him, and in the evening the children bathed him in a purling stream where the water seemed to boil from the ferocious heat and they put him to bed in the clubhouse wrapping him in cotton blankets, as if he were an infant and all the while he said not a word and they began to wonder if he would ever speak, if he even could speak for that matter. It was Peter who whispered one night after the old man had fallen asleep that perhaps he was an imbecile.

But this morning the old man smiled as Jimmy poked at his beard and he said in a robust voice, "Aw, it ain't so bad."

The children clapped in glee and Sue cried out, "He can talk!"

"I'm an old man," the old man said with a grin. "I can no longer tell when I'm asleep and when I'm awake."

But he was awake, and he proceeded to tell the

children his life story. He had been a circus performer in his youth and had traveled the world, a trapeze artist who amazed audiences with his soaring acrobatic skills. Over the years his reputation grew and soon he was sought after in every corner of the globe. He performed before heads of state in Europe. He ushered in periods of peace in the war-torn colonies of Central Africa. He dined with kings and queens on the banks of the Nile. He paid homage to Siberian tigers in the jungles of northern China. And in the Americas, he signed perfumed love letters from blushing young women who gazed at him with sultry eyes. It was one of these women whom he married—a ballerina from New York City—and together they formed their own act which they performed at arenas in San Francisco and Chicago and Boston and anywhere else if the money was good. But one day his wife was diagnosed with cancer and in a short time he found himself alone. He tried to continue his act by himself, but the crowds no longer came and soon he found himself without a job, washed up at the age of forty-two. He went to Georgia and found employment as a maintenance worker in a school for the blind. He worked there thirty years. How he ended up here with these bright and eager faces smiling down on him he had no idea. He had not felt like himself lately. Perhaps he had wandered away from the school grounds and gotten lost in town; it was so hot, you could not blame an old man for becoming disoriented in the heat.

The old man smiled again, and he showed his yellowed teeth and all the children were moved by his story. But as if to make up for his sad tale he rose from the bed and began to dance, slowly at first, then faster and faster, spinning around like a ballerina, hopping first on one leg then the other and he even did a cartwheel if you can imagine a seventy-two-year-old man doing such a thing. He must really have been something to see in his youth, Sally whispered. And all the while the old man was making funny faces like a clown and the children were laughing. But not Grace. She was sitting by the window, looking at the trees in the woods, the trees whose leaves were turning brown in the searing heat, and she did not laugh for she knew that the old man was lying.

It was the very next day that Grace put Sally in charge of the old man. Her family would be on vacation the next two weeks she told the startled girl, but the old man was recovering nicely, and she was certain Sally could take care of him.

"Where are you going?"

"The mountains."

"That sounds fine."

"Yes."

***

Time passes slowly when you're dreaming, the old man said once. Or was it time passes slowly when you're awake? Or time passes slowly when you're an old man? An old man who was dying. He had never said a word to Grace and yet he had said everything. He had never touched her and yet he had touched her heart. Her heart that was beating steadily like a drum. And it scared her now as she looked out over the diaphanous stream at the rocks in the clear water, rocks polished as smooth as dinosaur eggs. Time passing. Passing. She closed her eyes and she wanted it to stop, wanted it more than she had wanted anything in her short life, but it did not stop and she knew that it would never stop, and she did not know if she had the courage to confront the old man, but she knew that she must try.

When she returned to the cabin in the woods two weeks later she was filled with trepidation. She asked Sally how it had gone, and the strange girl simply smiled. They had taken care of the old man for awhile, she said, but he grew increasingly irritable because Grace was not there and when he snapped at little Jimmy one day they decided to leave him alone and Grace did not know what she would find there.

It turned out that she found nothing. The dusty clubhouse was empty. She went inside, her heart pounding, and she was afraid he would leap out at her from behind the door like a madman or slink out from under the bed like one of those multi-colored lizards in the woods, or rise up through a crack in the floorboards like a genii made of smoke and berate her for ever having left him. But he did not jump out, he did not slither, he did not ascend, he did not appear. She went over to the bed and touched the crumpled sheets on which he had slept. She did not know what to think. In her mind's eye, she saw him lying there, thin and frail, a mere wisp of a man, with a fragile intensity in his limpid eyes. She pulled back the sheets, hoping to find something there that would alleviate the ache in her heart, a note perhaps, or a gift however small, but she found nothing. The air in the clubhouse was oppressive and she went over to the window, her heart throbbing, tears welling in her eyes. She was about to throw open the curtains to let in a cool breeze that had unexpectedly arisen when she was startled by a sound at the door. Abruptly, she turned around.

A man stood in the doorway, a well-built man with thick eyebrows and dark, myopic eyes, a cigarette dangling from his fleshy lips. He exhaled a puff of smoke and then he took the cigarette from his mouth and flicked it away. His eyes slid over her. She heard the drone of the wind outside and it sounded like a swarm of bees. The man said nothing, and he continued staring at her and she did not like the gleam in his eyes and suddenly her eyelids felt heavy with sleep. It was the moment he had been waiting for. He took a step towards her and she saw the scar and she tried to cry out only no words came and before her eyes she saw her life shattering into a thousand fragments and still he said nothing only his ungual hands reaching out, his lips seeking her lips in the dimming light.

"No!" she cried, and she pushed past him into the heat of the woods. She ran to her house imagining his footsteps right behind her, only there were none and after what seemed an eternity she fell weeping into her father's outstretched arms.

At first, he did not believe her story, but when he saw the lacerations of time in her rheumy eyes he knew she was telling the truth.

"He's here," Mr. Lewis told a startled dispatcher, "and he's probably armed."

So, it came to be that two hours later the clubhouse in the woods was ringed with police, sharpshooters, reporters, politicians, megaphones blaring, "Mr. Sturdivant come out, come out with your hands up, you will get a fair trial, a court appointed lawyer is here to assist you." But he did not come out, would never come out. And when Officer Jones burst into the clubhouse at precisely five-fifteen that afternoon and saw the dead and rotting corpse swarming with maggots he could only mutter, "I'll be damned!"

The prisoner was buried the next day in a potter's field on the edge of town under a violet sky with only an old lady and a wayward tramp in attendance and shortly thereafter life returned to normal. Except for Grace, of course, whose life would never be the same. Eternity lasts forever, she said to me the very next morning, her head on my pillow, her pale-yellow eyes staring vacantly into space like two moonbeams, and never again would she return to the clubhouse in the woods, not out of fear of what she might find, but simply because she realized there was no longer anything there for her.

SEDGEFIELD'S DIARY

My name is Sedgefield—Thomas Sedgefield—or at least let me call myself that. I am fifty-eight years old, married, a small, thin man, with wavy black hair and gray eyes. I work as an accountant in an insurance firm in downtown Boston, a city in which I've spent my entire life.

"Sometimes faith becomes a belief in the absurd," my wife said to me one evening after dinner.

I didn't reply.

I was thinking about a presentation I was to deliver the next morning at the office. I didn't know what Marilyn was talking about, but as I thought more about it, later in the evening, the more I came to believe she was referring to me. The monotony of my existence. Not the fact that I exist, mind you, but that I don't actually do anything. Anything remotely interesting or unusual.

My days were repetitive. I took the subway to work at seven-thirty every morning and returned at six in the evening. I was greeted by my wife and we chatted about the day's events. While she cooked, I took care of leftover items from the office. After dinner, I settled into my leather easy chair. I was a voracious reader and often had my nose in a good mystery. I watched the eleven o'clock news most nights and then went to bed. I rarely did anything else. As far as anyone knew, Thomas Sedgefield was the most ordinary of men.

Except for one thing and that is detailing the entries in my diary. My diary is not a normal diary, that is, one that lists important events of the day. No, I take it upon myself to list every single event which has occurred.

Marilyn knows about my diary and though she thinks it odd—which it is—I think she sees it as a sign that I lack confidence. She points out I've never received a promotion at work, do next to nothing around the house, am chronically lazy, a never-ending procrastinator. What better way for me to seem important than to list an endless stream of my accomplishments! I admit that makes sense, I tell her. However, I do not think that explains the diary.

I have come to the conclusion that what drives me to write is precisely what my wife spoke of earlier: a belief in the absurd. I write down every detail of my life so that the diary becomes my life, that is, I ensure my immortality by detailing my existence. And if the truth be told, who amongst us does not wish to preserve the essence of his life? You might find it ironic that I, who am amongst the most insignificant of men, wished to preserve my insignificance for all to see. But such was the case.

I said earlier that I record every moment of my existence and the more discerning amongst you will undoubtedly have questioned the validity of that statement. Let me be absolutely clear: there was one exception. I did not write of what transpired in my mind while I slept, of my dreams or nightmares. My reasoning was as follows: the mind at night is a mysterious thing. It is prone to exaggeration if not outright falsification and I could not risk the diary being corrupted with erroneous entries. The accounting of my life must be both exact and precise. So, for nighttime a simple entry sufficed, for example: "November 1. Slept from 11:30 P.M. to 7:30 A.M."

I have been at work on my diary for nearly thirty years. Ten thousand nine hundred and five days. Each day's entries occupy approximately eight pages of a folio. I write at hourly intervals so that a single entry takes up about half a page. Each folio—they are black with red lettering on the spine—comprises a month of material. Three hundred and fifty-eight folios and counting.

I told my wife of my unusual habit before we married. (Pulling out a black diary once an hour and writing feverishly was hardly something I could have hidden from her for any length of time!) I believe she was amused by my antics, though as time went on, as she saw how much of my life was consumed by my bizarre habit, she grew concerned. Once she asked if I might consider consulting a therapist and even said she would accompany me. I told her I would look into it. I never did.

One Saturday after breakfast Marilyn was washing dishes and I was on the couch in the family room, trying to decide what to read next—I'd just finished the final volume of Proust's *Remembrance of Things Past*—when she cried out in agony and fell to the floor, clutching her right side. I rushed her to the emergency room. She was given a multitude of tests, but the doctors found nothing wrong. It was probably a case of indigestion, they said—and promptly sent her home.

One would have thought I had plenty to write about in my diary that day—and I did—but I was so concerned about Marilyn's condition that I forgot to pen a word. I awoke early the next morning after an endless night of troubled dreams. The reading lamp next to our bed was on, casting a pale light throughout the room. When I looked beside me I was surprised to see Marilyn thumbing through the most recent issue of *Better Homes and Gardens*. She looked at me and smiled. She told me she was feeling better and, in a moment, would get up and fix breakfast. I sighed in relief, and then—

And then I realized my error. The diary! You can imagine the shock-wave that surged through me. I'd been writing entries day after day for nearly thirty years and had never missed so much as an hour much less a day. And not only had I missed a day—it had been one of the most eventful days of my life! You might think the problem was not so bad, that I could reconstruct the previous day's events, which surely were burned into my memory, but such was not the case. Who can truthfully say that after a troubled night the recollection of the previous day's events has not been irrevocably altered? And so, it was with trepidation—in some way I would have to account for my inaction—that I opened the diary later that morning and prepared to make amends.

Imagine my surprise when I saw on pages 161-168 a complete account of the events of the day before. That it was in my own handwriting there was no doubt, just as there was no doubt, that I, Thomas Sedgefield, had not penned the words. Needless to say, I was dumbfounded.

It wasn't until later that afternoon that I was able to bring myself to re-examine the diary (meanwhile more entries had gone unwritten). I re-read what had been written the previous day. It seemed accurate enough— exactly as I remembered events unfolding. But the more I thought about it, the more I grew disturbed. No particular event was wrong, but the overall tone of the entries was different. Cold. Impersonal. A simple recitation of events. And it was then I realized what was wrong. If the entries were written by my hand—guided by my mind—they surely would have been full of the emotion of that day.

There was nothing to be done but wait. As you can well imagine, it was difficult for me to write anything the remainder of that day, though I persevered and wrote dutifully at the appointed times.

I became morose, ate sporadically, talked to no one. Marilyn asked what ailed me, but I made up excuses. The weather (it was getting cold). A touch of the flu (I ached and had chills). A general malaise (it had been a cold, rainy fall and I was depressed by dreary weather). I don't think she believed a word of it, though.

One day I tried an experiment. I decided that for a day I would write nothing in the diary. And I would wait to see what happened. I did little more than breathe that day, waiting for night to come. As far as I was concerned—as far as I wanted my diary to be concerned—I did nothing. I, Thomas Sedgefield, ceased to exist on the sixth of November.

Alas, when I opened the diary the next morning there were eight pages devoted to my inactivity of the day before. Each as accurate as had been the first entry I had not written. Which is to say not a word was in error. Only I could have written it. Only I did not remember having written it. Was it possible I was rising in the night to pen the words? I didn't think so—I would have remembered something, certainly, even if it was but a fading image from a dream.

There was really nothing that could be done about it, so I did nothing. I continued on as before, writing my entries dutifully every hour on the hour. Like a clock marking time. Every so often (I varied the time interval) I would skip a day—hoping to catch the diary off guard—but always the next morning the entries were there. Exact. Complete. Just as if I had written them. Once I went so far as to bind my feet together when I went to bed, so I would trip and wake up if I was sleepwalking, but it did not alter the result.

I do not believe in supernatural events. I do not believe in magical beings. But I could not explain what was happening without resorting to such an explanation. I reasoned as follows: if I (and not the diary) was writing the entries I would certainly have known it. I did not know it. Therefore, I was not writing the entries. No one else but my diary knew me well enough to construct such a precise accounting. It must have been the diary that was doing so. It was a reductio ad absurdum and I was left at a complete loss—when suddenly it hit me: I had been writing in my diary for so long—and in such detail—that I had transferred the essence of my mind to the diary, that is, that my life was to unfold in the diary whether I did anything about it or not.

This realization had unfortunate consequences. It meant that I no longer possessed free will, or—what amounted to the same thing—that something else controlled me, that is, that I no longer controlled my destiny.

That's wonderful, I thought to myself. *I could take myself out of time and be none the poorer for it!*

That evening, I told Marilyn everything. She did not laugh as I feared she would. On the contrary, she seemed concerned. Not about the unexplained diary entries, mind you, but about my sanity.

"Thomas," she said, glancing up from the red-and-white scarf she was knitting, "you need to take a break from that wretched journal."

That would never do, I reasoned. If I were to stop I would forever lose a part of me to the passage of time. It would be as if those unrecorded moments never had been (in a very real sense they never would have been). Nor could I allow the diary to do my work for me. It was there to help out, it was true, but I had no idea how long its good will would last.

And so instead of taking a break I redoubled my efforts. I resolved to record my life's events at thirty-minute intervals and in more detail than before. I would beat the diary at its own game.

The result was not what I expected. I awoke one morning to find to my horror that the coming day's entries had already been recorded. I was surprised not that the day's events were mapped out—this I expected, this I took as the logical consequence of preceding events—but that the events were exactly those I had planned. That was something I had never expected—could never have expected—and it cast a new light on what was happening.

When I got over the initial shock, I formulated a plan. Now that I thought of it, it would be a simple matter to trip up the diary. It was written that at two that afternoon I took an afternoon walk through the neighborhood across the bridge at Harper's Creek and over to Cassidy Park where I sat on a bench and gazed at passers-by for twenty minutes before returning home. All right, then. I would take an afternoon walk—as predicted—but I would deviate from the route. Instead of going west after crossing Harper's Creek I would go east which would take me though a hilly neighborhood and along a winding path to the local library.

I set out precisely at two. It was a pretty day in the month of February. The sky was blue with wisps of cumulus clouds floating lazily overhead. The air was crisp. A gentle breeze was blowing from the north. The road I was on wound through the neighborhood, past red brick houses with carefully manicured lawns, by a wooded area that served as a bird sanctuary, and up a steep hill to a place affectionately known as Lover's Heights. From here one had marvelous views of south Boston and of Harper's Creek below. I stayed a few minutes, mulling things over, and then I headed down the other side of the hill to the wooden bridge that crossed the creek.

But when the time came to go east instead of west I began to tremble. I realized if I deviated from my intended path—my path as already recorded in the diary—I would be committing the ultimate transgression, that is, my life as lived would not have corresponded to my life as recorded. And that would never do. In the end, the decision was simple: I turned west towards Cassidy Park. I fell in line with what was written.

Thomas Sedgefield, I thought as I approached the park, *is a most peculiar man. He is a man who has fallen in love with himself—there is no other way to explain his preoccupation with his own life. I would say he is like a five-year-old child who has never grown up. (What his wife sees in him is anyone's guess.) As for his desire to record every moment of his existence, it has been successful, but at what a price! The poor man has become a mere notation in the book of life. He has become a diary entry.*

Looking back, I see that that realization was the defining moment of my life. Before I would constantly worry lest I forgot to record any action. Afterwards I knew not only that they would be recorded, but that they would be recorded in advance.

And it was then that I began to look forward to the daily entries. They told me what to do, after all, which saved considerable time each day. Every so often I slipped in an entry or a comment on an entry—an embellishment, if you will, like a brushstroke upon a nearly completed section of a canvas—and that seemed to keep my mind content, at least for awhile.

It was a Sunday evening in early January of the following year. Marilyn and I were sitting on the couch in the living room. A fire was roaring, filling the room with warmth. "It no longer bothers me," I said. "The diary. I've come to accept it."

Marilyn was knitting a pair of booties for our first grandchild. (Did I forget to tell you that our daughter had given birth to a son only the week before? Such an important event—I don't know how it could have slipped my mind.)

I thought about what might happen next. What would I do when the last day of my life was predicted? What would I do if the end of the world was predicted? What would happen if I ripped a page from the diary or— shudder—burned the entire book! That I had done neither was a testament to the hold the diary had over me. Unfortunately, once one crossed such a line there was no going back.

And that—I feared—was what had happened to me. I had become as dependent upon my diary as I had upon the food which I consumed. In my attempt to preserve all that I am I had ended up losing all that I was.

There is more that could be said, of course, but let me leave things there. It must suffice to make one final point, a summation, if you will. Though the world is a harsh and sometimes confusing place, man has a tendency to adjust to a system, a way of life that enables him to cope with his surroundings, but by relinquishing control to a third party he runs the fearful risk of losing that which makes him unique. He has no longer adjusted to the system; he has become the system. At that point it is not even clear if he can properly be said to exist.

THE STRANGE STORY OF SAXON'S HILL

It was the spring of 1910. The Shenandoah Valley of Virginia. A town named Morgan's Creek, located on a branch of the Shenandoah River near Elkton. Population: two thousand.

The Shenandoah Valley was located in the western part of Virginia. It was the prettiest country one could imagine with lush farmland that seemed to stretch forever, the soil a rich dark loam that grew crops with little effort. The trees in the area were a mixture of maple, beech, oak, and pine. There were wildflowers of every conceivable variety. The Shenandoah River ran through the valley and drained much of the northwestern part of Virginia. It had two forks, the North and the South.

The town of Elkton was situated off South Fork. Near Elkton the South Fork entered a valley bounded on the east by the Blue Ridge Mountains and on the west by Massanutten Mountain, a dramatic landform that rose to over three thousand feet. The mountain loomed over the town of Morgan's Creek, which was situated in the middle of the valley at a bend in the river about ten miles from Elkton. A dark, forbidding place, Massanutten was known to shelter black bears, coyotes, and mountain lions, and was rumored to provide a haven for heathens, societal miscreants, and outlaws on the run.

Morgan's Creek was located at the base of a geological oddity named Saxon's Hill. The hill began as a nearly imperceptible rise near the north end of the valley and rose steadily like the tail of a dragon, taking a nearly vertical climb at one point and eventually reaching a height of three hundred feet. The hill was covered with thick vegetation and copses of pine trees. A path from the base wound to the top. It was often traveled, even though the trek was arduous, since the view from the top was spectacular: one could see the entire town, the river that snaked through the valley, and in the distance, the mists of the Blue Ridge Mountains.

No one knew for sure how the hill had received its name. There were several families named Saxon in the valley, but no one could recall the hill being part of their history. There was a famous gunslinger named Sexton—leader of the infamous Gang of Eight—who terrorized the valley in the early 1900's and was killed in a shootout on the hill top. And there was a rumor—quite prevalent at one time—concerning a sheep-herder named Saxon Parker, who owned grazing lands near the hill in the 1860's. A misanthropic old man who kept to himself, he had been involved in a bank robbery in 1866. The First Citizens' vaults were cleared out by two men who escaped from a prison in Charleston. While making their getaway, they had the misfortune of coming upon Mr. Parker at the base of the hill. He shot them dead—it was them or him, he said—and the money was reclaimed. Most of it, that is. A small portion was never found, though suspicion fell on Saxon himself. A finder's fee, perhaps. In any event, the matter was dropped, and people forgot about old Saxon until a year later when he was found hanging from the bough of an elm tree up on the hill. His throat was slashed, there were strange marks on his face and arms, and his body was drained of blood. And the rumor was this: Saxon made the whole story up! There never were any bank robbers, or rather, there was only one robber—the crazy man himself. Saxon was known as a teller of tall tales in the years before he withdrew from society. The law never took the rumor seriously, however, and Saxon's death was attributed to revenge. Even so, the rumor persisted, fueled in part by the fact that there was a third man who escaped shortly after the other two, and who stubbornly proclaimed their innocence. They'd all intended to travel south to Mississippi, he said.

My name is John Willis Round. I was born in Elkton, attended primary and secondary school there, and moved to Morgan's Creek shortly after I graduated. The events which follow occurred when I had just turned twenty-one. I was working on one of the many dairy farms that surrounded Morgan's Creek. I'd been a farmhand ever since I turned sixteen and had recently begun working summers for extra cash. Shortly after my eighteenth birthday, my father died from a sudden stroke and my mother turned to me to help provide for the family—the two of us, my three younger siblings and my father's aging parents (her own parents had perished in the influenza epidemic of 1884). I'd hoped to enter college that fall in Charleston and eventually become a doctor, but life has a way of intruding sometimes and there's really nothing a person can do.

I worked for the Elridge family. Ben Elridge was one of the wealthiest landowners in the valley, a man who was quite demanding but always fair. His wife, Betsy, was undoubtedly the nicest person in all of Morgan's Creek (her buttermilk biscuits, homemade sausages, grits, and hot apple pie greeted the farmhands many a morning). Alice, their daughter, was by far the prettiest young woman in Morgan's Creek. And the one with whom I was madly in love.

Alice Elridge was seventeen with shining dark eyes, rosy cheeks, and a captivating smile. She had a way of looking at me that made me turn away lest my eyes betray the passion that lurked within my soul. She was that beautiful. I'm sure she knew how I felt for I blushed when I was around her and stumbled over my words like a lovesick youth. I thought of her constantly, had trouble sleeping, and soon found myself unable to carry out my farm work with my usual alacrity. One day I could stand the stress no longer. My palms sweating, my hair unkempt, my eyes bloodshot from lack of sleep—I must have looked like an escapee from the county jail—I asked her out to the picture show. To my surprise she fairly shouted out the word, "Yes!" I never felt happier in all my life.

Three months later I asked Alice to marry me and she accepted. Her father was initially reluctant to permit the engagement—I'm sure he'd hoped to marry his daughter to a man with greater societal prospects—but after we convinced him of our mutual love, he begrudgingly agreed. I am convinced that Mrs. Elridge helped our cause.

There had been a strange series of animal deaths in Morgan's Creek that season: half-eaten carcasses of cows, sheep, and goats on several farms. No one had witnessed anything like it in the area, and it had the farmers on edge. The winter had been harsh, though, and most people thought the deaths were due to coyotes coming down off the mountains to feed.

Even with the sense of unease in the air, it was springtime and, as was always the case at that time of year, the aroma of wildflowers was intoxicating. Apple orchards were in full bloom, and smells in the valley made one feel as if one had died and been transported to heaven. Alice and I waltzed through those days, making wedding preparations and planning our honeymoon. We would marry in the town chapel and vacation for a week in Atlanta, Georgia.

It was not the wedding itself but an event which occurred the week before which was to change the course of my life. It was a Saturday morning. Alice called to tell me her wedding dress had arrived. It was more beautiful than she ever could have imagined. I asked if I could see her in it, but she refused. It was bad luck for a groom to see a bride in her gown before the wedding day, she said. I told her that was just seven days away. She laughed.

Of course, she was right to be cautious—I knew the unspoken rule—but even so I was powerless to resist the urge to see her. That evening I went over to her house on the north side of Morgan's Creek. For some reason my mind was ill at ease. I remember stumbling several times, even falling headlong into a puddle left by one of the recent spring rains. I must have looked like a vagrant when I reached the house—in addition to my tattered clothes I was dizzy and out of breath—and if someone had seen me pulling back the forsythia bushes to peer into the living room window I would have been apprehended on the spot!

There was another farmhand—Ned Chambers—who worked for Mr. Elridge during the spring planting season. I knew Ned only casually and he had always been pleasant enough around me. Once he had asked how I felt about the Elridge family. I thought it a strange comment, then realized he might be referring to Mr. Elridge's recent behavior—he had berated several of the farmhands for what he said was the poor quality of their work. When I mentioned the incident, Ned laughed and said he was thinking about the girl. This was about the time of my engagement and my feelings towards Alice must have been all too apparent. Ned seconded my pronouncement that Alice was quite beautiful.

Ned was tall and thin, about the same age as myself, with long, bony fingers and a ruddy complexion. He was a frequent patron of MC's Saloon and was considered a lady's man as well. I had heard several stories about his ability to drink late into the night; rumors of wild parties of a prurient nature were also prevalent.

This was the man I saw in the living room, stroking Alice's wedding dress, caressing her neck and shoulders, and laughing gaily. Alice was clearly amused by his attentions for her only response was to bat her eyes like an ingénue and swat playfully at his hand. Unfortunately, the window was closed so I could not hear what they were saying, but I could imagine every word.

As far as I could tell, Alice had never been close to Ned Chambers, nor any of the other farmhands, and I did not see how I could have been so deceived. Yet here was the evidence, right before my eyes. The playful banter. The light caresses. Now a hug and a tender kiss on the cheek!

I forced myself from the window and hurried home through sinister streets. A thick fog was closing in. I heard the throbbing of cicadas. The hoot of a night owl. I shuddered. Once home, I drowned my sorrows with a bottle of ale then went to bed where I tossed and turned for hours, agonizing over my plight, until at last sleep came upon me with its delicious forgetfulness.

The violent spring thunderstorms must have stirred up something from the abandoned paper mill upstream, for Morgan's Creek emitted an unbearable stench that sent more than two dozen people to the town infirmary. Three days of wild thunder, wicked lightning, and horrific mountain winds were followed by two days of a cold dreary rain. My soul was filled with foreboding. In retrospect, I should simply have gone to Alice and asked for an explanation, but I was afraid, I guess, of what she might say. So, I stewed in my own nightmarish vision of a tragedy that was sure to come. It also occurred to me that *Alice* could have come to *me*. This was—after all—the week before our wedding and much remained to be done. But she did not come and that only cemented my belief in her unfaithfulness.

It was on the morning of the sixth day—the day before our wedding—that I could stand the tension no longer and I decided to hike the winding path that led to the top of Saxon's Hill. It was a place I often went when I needed to be alone. I let Alice know where I was going, but I did not tell her why. Luckily, she did not ask.

The recent rains had ceased, though the sky was still a dark, forbidding gray. My mind wandering as I began the ascent, recent events unfolding once again before my eyes. The day before I had gone to see Alice. She met me at the door and ushered me inside as if nothing had happened. Her hair was pulled back in a bun and her pretty black eyes were shining brightly. I found myself making excuses for her recent behavior before I had even brought the matter up. She had always been so naïve; it was quite possible she had not realized what Ned's intentions were. Of Ned's desires, however, I was certain.

Alice choked up as she talked of the future that lay before us. "Tomorrow . . ." she said, and she looked away. If only she had known what that devilish farmhand intended. How he would pursue her, harass her, until she agreed to his desires—*oh God, please*, I thought, *I can't think of it anymore.*

My lower lip was twitching, and my right hand was shaking noticeably. Alice made no comment on my distress; she was in another world, thinking of our future happiness. And as I looked at her, I realized I loved her as much as ever. Yes, I concluded, it was just as I thought. It was Ned who had intentions on my lovely Alice. There was no complicity between them.

That evening I went to MC's Saloon, the town's only bar. I had been there several times and always found it a pleasant enough place—there was a band almost every night, and the food was quite good—but that night I found it dank and odorous, suffused with shadow, and filled with an air of dread. Maybe I had hoped to find Ned there to confront him. I don't know. I sat at the bar for over an hour—drinking and watching and waiting—but he did not appear. Along one side of the room was a stage. I saw a banjo, a ukulele, and three acoustic guitars. In front of the stage was a dance floor, now empty.

It was growing late when the man seated next to me at the bar tugged on my sleeve. I turned and found myself facing a congenial-looking man of about forty with a plain, round face and dark-brown eyes. He was shabbily dressed in an old plaid shirt, weather-beaten Stetson, tan pants, and leather boots that could have used polishing. He was sipping a drink he held in his left hand.

"Yer friend's a pincher," he said. There was a strange gleam in his eye as he added, "and he always gets what he's after."

I was struck dumb as you can well imagine. The man chuckled and said, "Naw, I don't know who yer here for exactly. But I see the look, and it's always the same."

I'd lived my entire life in Morgan's Creek and I knew almost everyone in town, but I did not recognize this man.

"You from around here?" I asked.

"Nope," he said. "Just passin' through."

"Where you from?"

He paused. "Does it matter?"

"You a drifter?"

"Could call me that, I suppose."

Our conversation was interrupted by the strumming of guitars. A bluegrass band had taken the stage: three men and a woman, all in their late twenties. The men were nondescript, but the woman was a real beauty with bright blue eyes and luxurious long, blond hair. There were several minutes of playful banter with the crowd. Then the band struck up a raucous number and moments later people were dancing in front of the stage.

"I'm lost," I said. "At least I feel that way."

"No use worryin' 'bout the gal," he replied. "What'll be'll be."

A true enough statement, to be sure, but it did nothing to assuage my fears.

The dancers were a young crowd. They looked happy and carefree. *I was like that once*, I thought. It was growing steadily smokier in the room and the lights on the stage cast bizarre shadows on the walls. I looked over at my companion. The lights were playing on his face, a kaleidoscope of shifting colors.

The man must have been able to read my mind. "They don't appear to have a care in the world, do they?" he said.

"No," I said. "They don't."

"Their days are numbered, though," he laughed.

"Like swine." And he slapped his thigh as if he'd said something very funny.

Chills were running down my spine. This man wasn't from around here. Nor anywhere close by.

He tossed down the rest of his drink and then he was gone, to my utmost relief.

That was what I recalled as I began the trip to the top of Saxon's Hill. The climb was difficult but uneventful and by the time I was halfway up I felt noticeably better. The air was cooler. A gentle breeze stirred the branches of the elms and the pines.

I heard a woodland creature rustling in the tangled vegetation up ahead. I must have approached too closely, for it scampered away. It made an odd whimpering sound as it retreated, unlike the vocalization of any creature with which I was familiar.

The path's final stretch was muddy, and I had to detour to make progress. At one point I stumbled over the root of an oak tree and went sprawling. I cursed my clumsiness.

As I was nearing the top I heard voices. The rain had only recently stopped, and I couldn't imagine why anyone else would have made the trek up. I stopped and listened closely. There were two men—possibly three—and their voices were raspy, the diction odd. I didn't think they came from the valley. The vocalizations of one of the men were unusual: bizarre guttural sounds and weird simpering noises interspersed with an occasional moan.

The top of Saxon's Hill was a glade about fifty yards across surrounded on three sides by trees and heavy underbrush. The fourth side was cleared away and afforded magnificent views of Morgan's Creek and the mountains in the distance. It was a beautiful yet lonely place, the perfect spot when one needed solitude. I was only twenty yards from the top, but already I could tell something was wrong. The pines were swaying and the bushes moving eerily as if possessed by unnatural powers. The soil itself seemed to exhale an intoxicating fragrance.

Now I was certain. The voices belonged to two men

and they were arguing. Or rather one was arguing with the other who was making childish whining sounds in reply.

I did not dare enter the glade from the main path. My instincts told me an evil had been committed and I had no desire to walk into the middle of a crime. If I had been thinking clearly, I would have returned to Morgan's Creek for help.

There was a second entrance, one which few people knew of, but that I had used with Alice when we were courting. The path which led to it was overgrown and made for a challenging climb, but it opened onto the western part of the glade where the views of the valley were the most splendid. I veered off the main path, moving cautiously so as not to be heard in my approach. I pushed through tangles of vines and heavy vegetation. Every few feet I stopped and listened. Still the voices came, hoarse and raspy and downright ghostly. I hoped the men were too preoccupied with their own activities to be aware of my approach.

The path opened onto the glade in an area thick with thorn bushes and scrubby pines. I clung to one of the branches, peering out over the glade at one of the strangest sights I had ever seen. Two men were standing no more than a dozen feet from me. Their bodies emitted a malodorous stench and their faces were covered with beads of sweat. The first man was large, ill-shaven, with thick-black hair, deep-set dark-brown eyes, and enormous ears like those of a gargoyle. He was dressed in baggy dark clothes. In his left hand he clutched a knife, which he was sharpening by drawing across a stone. The other man was small, with a square face, curly brown hair, a grizzly beard, and oversized ears like his companion. A patch covered his right eye and his left stared wildly.

The top of Saxon's Hill was not as I remembered it. Formerly a lush green place, it was now barren and empty. It resembled a naked plateau, a nightmarish otherworldly place, an arid gray desert sprawling open to the sky as if acid had consumed it. The large man was shouting orders. The other was staring at him in an almost comical fashion. There was a fire blazing off to one side. Two knapsacks were on the ground near the fire and a small copper kettle and something else on the other side—a sleeping bag, perhaps—but it was difficult to make out what it was in the smoke that was rising.

Because of the recent rains, the branches I was clinging to were slippery. At one point I lost my grip, fell forward, and tumbled into the glade. A moment later I felt the cold steel blade of a knife against my throat. The one-eyed man was glaring at me. I raised my hands to my chest, palms up. I lost consciousness when a sharp pain shot through my skull.

When I came to I found myself seated beside the fire. My head ached, and I saw a rock a few feet away with blood on it. My blood, no doubt. I shuddered. My arms were bound behind my back and my mouth was gagged. The large man was tending the fire. The second man was lying on the ground and appeared to be asleep. The copper pot—suspended over the fire by a stout branch—was bubbling.

All this was unsettling enough, but when I looked to my left—at the fire that was blazing—I received the shock of my life. On the other side of the crackling fire I saw the prostrate body of Ned Chambers! His throat had been slashed and blood still seeped from the wound.

The man saw me staring at the body and he chuckled. "That fellow's not dead yet, but he will be soon," he said. And then he roared with laughter.

I struggled to free my arms, but the bonds held fast. I turned from side to side, my eyes sweeping across the barren wasteland. I saw that I was still at the western end of the glade, right up against the thorn bushes that lined the glade's edge.

"Name's Frank," the man continued. "Pleased to meet ye."

I tried to reply, but the gag muffled the sound. Frank noticed my attempt to speak and he bent to remove it. "One cry and I'll kill ye," he said and then laughed again, a hideous demonic howl. "I reckon we're far from civilization up here, ye remember that."

The other man had awoken and was sniffing at the ground like a dog.

"Don't ye mind Abe," Frank said. "His head's a little queer."

A look of puzzlement must have crossed my face for he added, "My companion ain't too bright. Though he does like humans, if ye know what I mean."

The horror was all too clear: the roaring fire, the warm body of Ned Chambers, the dumb brute whimpering like an imbecile, drool dripping from his chin. Frank pulled out his knife and held it up and examined the blade. "Gawd, it's sharp," he said. "And Abe, I think he's hungry." He laughed once more; I thought he would never stop laughing.

"You killed him?" I was staring at Ned's body.

"Yessir," Frank said. "A right fine killin'."

"May God have mercy on your soul."

"I reckon we ain't of Gawd's world."

I swooned and for the second time that afternoon lost consciousness.

When I came to for the second time, Frank was tending the fire. He was speaking in hushed tones but appeared to be talking only to himself. I couldn't make out a word he was saying. What was I to do? I was at the edge of the glade, right up against the thorn bushes that hid the path I had taken. I realized the bushes were my only hope. I pressed my bonds into the thorns and slowly—I hoped imperceptibly—moved my wrists back and forth. It was all I could do not to cry out from the pain. I felt the coldness of blood against my skin as it dripped down my wrists and onto the ground. I prayed that the breeze didn't send the scent Abe's way. It was hard work, but eventually the bonds loosened.

It was then I noticed that the sky was darkening.

"Ahem." It was Frank. "How ye doing?" His eyes gleamed darkly, watching me. "Aw now, cheer up. No good to be 'fraid."

"Where are you from?"

"What's it to ye?"

"You're not from around here," I said. "You sound mighty odd."

He eyed me curiously.

"As a matter of fact, I think I was just talking to a friend of yours, back in town."

"Guess it don't matter," he said and shrugged. He pointed up at the sky. "See that point of light?"

"No," I said. "It's cloudy."

He scoffed. "That's 'cause yer blind. Ye can't see a thing. Never mind. The fourth planet from Sirius, the Dog Star. That's where we come from." He slapped his side and roared with laughter.

I felt the gentle buffetings of the gathering wind and heard the rumble of a steady but distant thunder. I looked up at the sky. "It's about to rain," I said. "A thunderstorm. By the looks of the clouds it will be a good one."

"Naw," Frank said. "It'll pass."

"I don't think so," I said. "You two came to the wrong place. This hill is spooked."

Frank pulled out his knife again and came over to me. There was an ugly gleam in his right eye. "What do ye mean by that?"

"Nothing," I said. My heart was pounding. "I just think it's gonna rain, that's all."

"Hey, Abe," Frank called to his cyclopean companion. "Do ye want to start with this one?"

Abe rose from the ground and lurched over to me. He was howling like a hyena and saliva was pouring from his mouth.

All the while the sky grew darker. I heard the distant rumble of thunder.

"He was my friend," I said.

"Who—that?" Frank indicated Ned's body, which was still dripping blood.

I nodded.

"Should take more time to pick yer friends."

"What do you mean by that?"

"Don't mean nothin'. It's just what I said."

It was noticeably darker now. Peals of thunder

echoed in the distance and lightning shimmered across the valley. Pine trees swayed eerily. It was then I realized that the birds had grown silent.

"You know what they say," I continued.

"Naw, I don't know what they say," Frank mocked. "What do they say?" He had begun dragging the knife over the stone.

"Any man who kills on Saxon's Hill is a dead man."

Frank bellowed with laughter. "Why's that?"

"Because this hill has *eyes*. It sees, and it knows—and it takes revenge."

"Shut up!" Frank slapped my face and I felt blood on my lip. At the sight of the redness, Abe went wild.

"You didn't have to kill him." I forced the words through my swollen lips.

"That's what we're here for," Frank said. "And that's the way it always will be—at least until yer sun explodes." He scowled. "Besides, Abe's gotta eat." Lines of anger were etched into his face. I didn't know how far I could push him. "Who are ye to tell us who we can kill?" he continued. "Yer acquaintance be damned. I bet ye didn't even know him. Tonight, it's ye and him and Abe here, and in the mornin' we be gone. Into them hills yonder"—he indicated the mountains beyond the valley—"and what be that to ye?"

He raised the knife. His madman's eyes were only inches from mine and I felt his rancid breath on my face.

I didn't have time to reply, for at that moment it came. The loudest clap of thunder I'd ever heard; it nearly split my ear-drums open. Bolts of lightning shot across the darkness and, out of the macabre silence that hung over the valley, I heard a horrible wail. Frank looked up and for the first time that afternoon—maybe for the first time ever—there was fear on his face. It was then I realized I had to strike—it was now or never.

But how? My bonds, though loosened, still held me. With a grimace, I thrust my wrists into the thorn bush. I cried out as the thorns bit into my skin. Frank must have heard for he spun around and looked at me in alarm. He was hovering over me, the wild lightning illuminating the astonishment on his face. With a triumphant shout, I burst the bonds which fell harmlessly away. I swung my legs up and hit Frank hard in the chest with both feet. He fell backwards into the fire. The knife clattered onto the ground. He must have struck the copper kettle and been knocked senseless for he did not move.

I picked up the knife and watched in horror as the dancing flames consumed him. His wild hair was ablaze. His eyes, glassy and terror-stricken, stared up at the dark sky which was crisscrossed with streaks of lightning. I shuddered, realizing he had not been knocked unconscious, but was stunned and paralyzed by fear.

And then I was upon him. Three times I plunged that instrument of death into his chest. I watched in revulsion as he gasped and lay still. When I was certain he was dead, I turned to confront the other one. But Abe was nowhere to be seen. I looked over at the dying fire, saw Ned Chamber's withered corpse. I remember calling out: "May God rest his soul!" as I collapsed on the ground and lay still.

It was there that they found me. The clouds had lifted, the sky reddening in the west. I was sputtering nonsense, they said, something about wind and lightning and rain. The bodies of the two dead men were beside me. One—Frank's—had been burned to a crisp; the remains of his face still registered astonishment. The corpse of the second man—Ned—was strangely white and was later found to be devoid of blood. Only I knew the horrible fate which had befallen him.

I was taken to the infirmary where I slept for three days and three nights.

It was the morning of the fourth day when I sat upright and slung my legs over the side of the bed. A nurse was seated at a table with her back towards me. When she heard me rise, she turned and smiled.

There was an inquiry, as was required in these sorts of cases, but my account of events was accepted and that was the end of the matter. Alice and I married six months later and a year after that moved to Charlottesville to start a new life together.

***

That, anyway, is the story I told Alice a decade later as we sat before a roaring fire in the living room of our brick home on the outskirts of Charlottesville.

"Yes," she said lovingly as she caressed the back of my hand, recalling those days from long ago. "Your courage is what drew me to you, John. That and your eternal handsomeness." She paused. "But—I *know* all this. Why do you bring it up after all this time?"

No one can possibly know the horror that plagued me through those long and lonely years as I relived the tragic events at Morgan's Creek, the wretched insomnia that hounded me, haunted me, persecuted me, when I dared not lay my wracked body to rest for fear of vile images that would prey upon my mind. No one—no one!—can imagine.

I sighed as I felt the weight of oppression full upon my shoulders. "Because none of it is true," I said finally—forcefully—and I continued with haltering words, "It was I who killed Ned Chambers, killed him out of anger and rage, a seething jealousy, for he had dared woo the woman I loved. I could not bear the thought that he might one day come between us. I struck him down on Saxon's Hill, mutilated the body where it fell at my feet. There were no marauders, no assaults. I was never in any danger. The other man they found me with was a drifter I killed in an attempt to cover up my crime."

And as I gazed at Alice's horror-stricken face, I said the only words that would come to my lips, words that had been echoing in my skull for so many years, "How will you ever forgive me!"

THE LAKE OF FLIES

It was never determined precisely when Max decided to murder his ex-roommate from college. But when the deed was done it set in motion a chain of events which, like the ticking of a fine Swiss watch, was later seen to be inevitable. Perhaps the whole sordid affair was inevitable, triggered when Max met Stan on the quad of Xavier University, or the moment Max was born, or the moment the universe came into being 13.8 billion years ago. Or even before that time.

***

Max lived in northern Minnesota. He was thirty-four years old. A handsome man, solidly built, with dark-brown hair and engaging eyes. He was a canoe guide with an outfitter in Ely. It was while attending a conference on wilderness medicine that he ran into Stan, whom he had not seen since college. Stan was six months younger. Wiry frame, blond hair, bushy eyebrows. There was a ragged scar on his neck, the result of a motorcycle accident when he was eighteen. Though they'd graduated a dozen years earlier, they recognized each other at once. Stan said he was a rehabilitation therapist at a hospital in Milwaukee. He smiled knowingly when Max told him his occupation. It was at dinner that evening when Max suggested Stan visit later that summer. He would show him the crystal lakes of the Boundary Waters. Stan jumped at the opportunity; he could use a break from work, he said.

Max and Stan roomed together at Xavier for two years before Stan moved in with Sally. Even back then Stan expressed interest in accompanying Max on one of his excursions to the Boundary Waters area, trips which occurred every August before Fall semester began. Unfortunately, they never found the time.

At over one million acres, the Boundary Waters area in northern Minnesota contains boreal and hardwood trees, granite rock formations as well as volcanic and sedimentary rocks. Bears, moose, beavers, bald eagles, and loons all call the place home. With over ten thousand lakes and nearly as many hiking trails, it is a recreational paradise.

***

Max and Stan headed out from Ely in *Sandy*, the birchbark canoe Max had lovingly constructed back in '93. The vessel was sixteen feet long, narrow-bottomed, with a well-rounded bilge, and gently flaring topsides. It was fourteen inches deep at the center, with a prow height of twenty-four inches. A real beauty.

They slipped into the water at Newfound Lake, a long, thin body of water that emptied into horseshoe-shaped Sucker Lake. They crossed into Canada at Prairie Portage, on the western end of Sucker, then headed northeast through Birch Lake, Carp Lake, and Sheridan Lake. A portage—the trail they'd take from one lake to the next—from Sheridan led to a string of smaller lakes, known as the Man Chain. Max's friend was exhausted when they reached That Man Lake by nightfall.

Max and Stan beached their canoe on one of six islands which dotted That Man Lake, a peanut-shaped isle, with birch trees on one end and sandy beach on the other. Two single-man tents were up in twenty minutes. Then they fired up the Coleman. While black bean chili was cooking, Max took his hand-ax and cleared shrub from around the campsite. Stan gathered wood for a fire.

Max heard the thrumming bass of bullfrogs. On the eastern shore, he spied a quartet of loons after their own dinner. A school of small, dull-gray fish was visible in the shallow water off to his right. The pristine lakes of the Boundary Waters teemed with walleye, pike, bass, and trout. Later he would go fishing.

Not looking where he was going, Max tripped over a branch and went sprawling. The loons must have seen him—or heard the branch snapping in two—for they took off, slowly rising into a deep-blue Minnesota sky, a soaring, graceful flight.

After dinner, Max and Stan spoke of the week ahead. Their intent was to use this site as a base camp from which to explore the other lakes in the chain: No Man Lake, This Man Lake, and Other Man Lake. There was a large island with high, steep slopes at one end of Other Man Lake which afforded magnificent views. And lowland to the north of This Man Lake where they would likely see kingfishers, beavers, and river otters. Max told Stan it would be a week he would never forget.

***

The night was peaceful and still. Around 6 A.M., Max awoke to the dulcet sounds of loons as they settled on the lake in search of food.

Max opened his tent and stepped outside. The air was cool. No sign of life from his friend's tent. He walked the thirty yards to the opposite end of the island—the rocky end. He looked out over the lake, at the rising sun that mingled mists of grey and gold with the lake's blue waters. He mimicked the call of the loons, but they paid no heed.

"What you up to?" It was Stan.

Max turned around, startled.

"Thought you were asleep."

"Been up for over an hour. Thought I smelled a bear."

He hadn't, of course. Max would have smelled it as well. The scent of bear was not something you ever forgot.

***

Max had been sixteen years old. He and his father were canoeing for the first time in the Boundary Waters. They camped on an island in Emerald Lake, so named because of the greenish tint of its waters. It was their third day out. The man at the outfitter agency told them bears had been spotted in that area the previous month, and to take precautions. Max's father said that meant to camp on an island far from shore where they wouldn't be bothered. But it hadn't worked out that way. Max awoke in the middle of the night and smelled the most God-awful stench. He lay quivering in the darkness, too afraid to call out to his father. He heard a crunching sound as some creature rambled through the camp site. The smell grew stronger until Max felt stale breath upon him. He must have fainted for the next thing he knew it was no longer night. And the smell was gone.

At breakfast the next morning Max told his father what had happened. The crazy old man hadn't smelled a thing, had slept through it all! Max's story was corroborated later that day when they spied a young bear wadding along the shore. His mother would be near, Max's father said. And they wouldn't want to mess with her.

They left Emerald Lake, taking a long portage that led to Plough Lake. No signs of bears, though they did see a variety of waterfowl and a family of otters. The sky was deep and blue. A gentle breeze rustled the leaves of birch trees that lined the shore. It may have been at that moment when Max realized this was the place for him.

***

Max and Stan's destination that day was the third lake in the chain: This Man Lake. It had the longest portage of any of the lakes in the chain, about half a mile. And it would take them over hilly, rocky terrain.

They ate a simple breakfast of eggs and home fries, washed up, then loaded Sandy with the day's provisions. At precisely 7:45 they embarked, their paddles slipping noiselessly through calm waters.

"Man, this is the life," Stan said when the island was fifty yards behind them. "Should have done this years ago." He paused. "How long you been a guide out here, Maxwell?" Stan had always called Max by that name, even back in college. Max hated it then. He hated it now.

"Coming up on five years," he replied. "And, yeah, it's the lifestyle for me. Peace. Calm. Tranquility."

"And women."

Max shot him a puzzled look.

"Oh, come on." Stan laughed. "Sought-after tour guide. Out here away from it all. Must be lots of time for foolin'."

"Not so much." Max paused. "I miss Sally."

The canoe lurched forward as Max gave it a series of deep, strong strokes.

Stan looked across the lake wondering whether he should bring the subject up. Then he realized Max already had. "Sorry about stealing your girl," he said. "You forgive me?"

"Sure."

"If I hadn't, you'd never have found Emma, you know. And she's some gal."

"*Was* . . ." Max emphasized, "until Jack took her away."

Stan hadn't known. He shrugged. "Not my fault if you could never hold onto a woman." Stan meant it as a joke, but Max didn't laugh.

He felt anger slowly beginning to burn, and he

changed the subject. "You and Sally doing well?"

"We get along."

Max detected a frown.

"And the kids? There's two of them, right?"

Stan nodded. "Jennifer and Susan. Six and ten. Quite a handful—both of them." He paused. "You know, I love my life, wouldn't trade it for the world, but I envy yours. Heading out to a lake whenever you want. Must be nice."

"It *is* nice."

The canoe was approaching the eastern end of That Man Lake. They beached her, consumed a pouch of trail mix, and cut through a copse of cedar trees to begin the portage to No Man Lake. The trail was smooth and sandy, level all the way, about a quarter of a mile. When No Man Lake came into view Stan gasped. It was one of the prettiest lakes in the region. A small, nearly circular body of clear-blue water, with birch and cedar trees lining the shore.

They made their way across in ten minutes, aided by a gentle south-westerly wind, and landed on the northern portage that led to This Man Lake. This trail was three feet wide and well-marked. Max took the backpack and paddles. Stan shouldered the fifty-pound canoe. Maple and birch trees loomed skyward in a canopy that turned daytime into night.

Along the way they saw red squirrels, robins, wrens, and red-winged blackbirds. They inhaled the aroma of fallen leaves and of wild aster blossoms. They heard a yowling sound off in the distance which Max did not recognize. A lynx, perhaps. They were rare in these parts, but Max had come across one once or twice. There were blackberry bushes along one side of the trail. Max said they needed to be on the lookout for bears who'd been spotted earlier that season.

The trail rose slowly at first, then became steep and rocky, leveling off at a height of about fifty feet. At that point the trees thinned out and they could see clearly to This Man Lake, about a quarter mile away.

Max saw something else.

Off to his left, about two hundred yards away, was a small lake, perfectly circular, and surrounded by small pines and brush.

"What's that?" he said, motioning Stan to halt. Stan lifted the canoe from his shoulders and set it on the side of the trail.

Max opened the backpack and took out a map. They'd gone maybe halfway along the portage. At that spot there was a small unnamed lake, but, according to the map, it was further inland. Perhaps this was an unknown lake?

"Let's investigate," Max said.

He took the backpack, which held water, trail mix and the ax, and headed off down the path, using the ax to clear the way. Stan followed at his heels, eager to check out the unknown as well.

It was perhaps thirty minutes later when the foliage thinned, and they found themselves at the edge of a granite slope which led to the lake below.

The lake was about thirty yards wide. It was surrounded by granite rock that rose at a steep angle, making access to the water impossible. It looked surreal, sunlight glistening off the granite as if it were polished glass. The only reason they'd seen the lake was because of the height of the trail at that point of the portage.

It was a drop of perhaps thirty feet to the water's surface. But how Max would have loved to reach the water! It was coal-black and seemed to undulate, slowly rising and falling as if it were a living, breathing thing.

It was.

Pulling out the binoculars, Max saw that the surface of the lake was covered by a thick layer of flies. There must have been hundreds of thousands, feeding on the kettle's algae. The sun reflecting off the flies' wings made the surface resemble a gigantic compound eye. A glistening ommatidium. Max gazed upon it, mesmerized. He felt as if he was peering into the mind of an intelligence that had taken over the lake and was lying in wait. He did not know for what. But it seemed to be drawing him in.

"I know it's none of my business," Max said abruptly, "but are you and Sally having problems?"

"Let's just say it's not what it was, but I make do—if you know what I mean."

Stan smiled, and Max's anger, which had been steadily brewing, reached a crescendo.

"Here," Max said, handing the binoculars to Stan. "Take a look."

Stan scooted to the edge of the granite slope, as far as he deemed safe, and crouched down on his knees, peering through the binoculars at the dark mass below. "Good Lord!" he exclaimed.

The blunt end of the ax down came down hard against Stan's skull. He slumped forward without a sound, his head striking the granite. Max stared at him awhile, the ax poised to strike a second blow if needed. It wasn't.

Max put his right foot against Stan's shoulder blades and pushed. The dead man tumbled down the embankment, landing with a splash in the black waters, scattering thousands of flies which rose up in a huge dark cloud.

A faint grayness crept across the once blue sky.

***

Back in Ely the next evening, Max consoled a bereaved Sally Hobart who'd flown in from Milwaukee. Sally was a petite woman with luminous light-green eyes and shoulder-length auburn hair, finely-drawn features, immaculate skin. It was easy to see why Max had been so taken with her.

But now there were bags under her eyes and tears were flowing down her cheeks.

They'd been on This Man Lake when it happened, Max told her. Stan spotted something in the water and leaned over the canoe to get a better look. Too far as it turned out. The vessel overturned. The edge of the canoe struck Max on his head, leaving him dazed. That was all it took. Stan must have panicked, flailed about. There was nothing Max could have done. When he came to his senses, Stan was nowhere to be seen. This Man Lake was wide and long—and about a hundred feet deep. It would be searched, of course, but they might never find the body. She needed to be prepared for that.

When he'd finished telling Sally what had happened, he took her hands in his.

"I'm here if you ever need something," he said. "You know that, right?"

He felt a squeeze.

"Thanks." She smiled.

***

Max wrote to Sally several times over the next few months to see how she was getting along. She told him it was hard, but that she was doing okay. He told her anecdotes about the crazy times he and Stan had back in their college days, things he thought she'd appreciate. He even joked once about how after Stan had stolen her away he'd told Stan he'd never be forgiven. Stan had worried about that, she told Max. About his taking her away from Max. Stan hadn't wanted it to ruin their friendship—it had for a time—but he couldn't deny what had blossomed between him and Sally.

Max felt rage burning within his breast when he read those words. Only time would tell, he thought, if a different flower now would bloom.

***

Max didn't hear from Sally again until nearly a year had passed. Then one evening in early August he got a call. The first anniversary of Stan's death was a week away, she said. She asked if he would take her out to the lake where the accident had occurred.

Of course, Max told her. It was the very least he could do. The Man Chain was one of the most tranquil areas in the Boundary Waters. Perhaps they could camp for a day or two.

Sally asked again, her voice trembling: how had it happened?

Max felt himself swoon as he tried to recall what he had initially told her. It seemed so long ago. There had been a storm, he lied. He remembered feeling surprised, for storms rarely occurred in the morning hours. When the dark clouds gathered, they were on the portage that led to Other Man Lake. The air was heavy and moist. They never should have gone onto the lake, he said, but Stan insisted. Max would never forgive himself for agreeing. When they were three-quarters of the way across, the winds began to blow. The canoe was swaying and . . . He stopped. It was too horrible to recall.

There was a long pause. Then: "Didn't Stan die on This Man Lake? That's what the police said. That's the lake I've imagined for nearly a year. That's the lake I want to see."

"Yes, that was the one," Max replied, his voice tense. "As I said, everything is all jumbled up."

"And they didn't say anything about a storm. One would think that day would be seared in your memory."

"Yes," he said. "I guess I'm confused."

There was a long pause. "I'm confused, too," she said.

Max felt his heart flutter. No, he'd never gotten over Sally, nor—he felt sure—had she gotten over him.

***

"It was near here," Max said as they reached the western end of This Man Lake. He was in the rear of the canoe. Sally was in the bow, her paddle low in the water. "I remember those sun-bleached cedars along the southern bank. There are no islands on this part of the lake and we were far from shore. Stan didn't have a chance."

She turned around to face him. He saw that her eyes were glazed.

"I know how hard this must be for you, Sally."

The air was deathly quiet. A flock of cedar waxwings spangled the sky, their yellow and blue tail feathers lit by sunlight. Max pulled his paddle from the water and laid it flat across the hull. "It's beautiful out here, isn't it? So peaceful. So still."

"Yes."

"Sally . . ." He reached for her hand, but she pulled it back.

"I know what you're thinking," he said, "and I suppose you're right."

"What am I thinking?"

"That with Stan gone I'm hoping we can rekindle what we had."

She bit her lip, stifling words.

"Maybe I need to forget about the past," he said. "But I can't."

Her composure vanished.

"I've lost my husband," she said, her voice scalding like a hot iron. "My children have lost their father. My life this past year has been a living hell."

"Sally," Max began, his voice steady. "I'm not sure how to say this, but, on our trip out here, your husband told me what was going on."

She looked at him quizzically. "What do you mean?"

"He told me he was having an affair. I hate to be so blunt. I'm sorry."

She laughed. "There was no affair."

"He said things weren't good between the two of you, but that it didn't matter anymore."

"That's not much to hang an accusation on," she scowled. "Look, Stan's father died that year. Stan was having a horrible time of it. They'd been estranged. Stan was hounded by guilt. Of course, things were difficult between us—but that doesn't mean Stan was off having flings. It would have been the furthest thing from his mind."

"I know how this must hurt," Max said. "I can't believe he treated you like that. You deserve better."

"I'm flattered," she said. The look she shot Max was cold.

"I'm sorry. I didn't mean it that way."

It was then that Max saw the moose. It was wading along the southern shore. A magnificent creature, with a light brown body, elongated head, beautiful antlers. Moose were the largest mammals in the Boundary Waters. Adults stood six feet tall at the shoulder and weighed up to a thousand pounds.

"Look at those antlers," Max crooned. "Did you know that male moose have the largest antlers of any creature in the world?"

She turned her back and began paddling once again. "Let's get out of here," she said.

***

They were halfway across the level portage to No Man Lake, when Max gave a start. He laid the canoe down.

"Is something wrong?" Sally asked.

Max was looking off to the right. At something. Sally couldn't see exactly what.

"No," he said. "Nothing's wrong."

"You look apprehensive," she said. "What are you staring at?"

"It's a small lake," he said. "Nothing special. I was there once, that's all." He was fidgeting nervously with the backpack straps, and she noted that he had begun to perspire.

A chill swept over her then as she realized what must have happened. The clues were all around her. How could she have been so blind? "You were there once," she said. "With my husband?"

"No," Max lied. "It was another time. Don't remember exactly when. But I think it was—after."

"It seems to trouble you." She eyed him closely, noticed that his face was flushed. "I'd like to see it. If you don't mind."

He shrugged. He wiped the sweat from his brow and took a drink from his water bottle.

The foliage had grown up thickly over the past year. Max pulled the ax from the backpack and began chopping away.

"I like mysterious, out-of-the-way places, don't you?" she said.

Max didn't like the sound of her voice. It had a harsh

edge. Or was that just his imagination?

Thirty minutes later they reached No Name Lake. The canopy opened abruptly on their approach, and the clearing shimmered beneath a glaring sun. Max's heart was pounding. His eyes were fixated at a spot on the opposite side of the lake. He could not bring himself to look at the water below.

"It's an odd place," Sally said. "Not like the lakes we've visited. And it smells strange. A musty, decaying odor. Wouldn't you agree?"

Max turned to look at her. His teeth were clenched.

He put down the ax and sniffed at the air. "I don't smell anything odd," he said.

He crouched down at the edge of the granite slope that led down to the lake. He peered at brackish waters.

"The flies," he said in surprise. "They're gone."

"Flies?"

"Thousands of them. Big black monsters. Covered the surface. I'd never seen anything like it."

"I thought you said there was nothing special about this place?"

Max stood, hands at his sides, and turned slowly around. The dark hollows of Sally's eyes looked strange and terrible, and her hardened expression was not something he had ever hoped to see.

"What are you implying?" he said.

There was a flash of metal in the light of a blinding sun as Sally picked up the ax.

Max's thoughts dissolved in a maelstrom of panic. "Sally, please. I can explain—"

As his body tumbled into the water, the flies descended from a copse of pines on the other side of the lake. Thousands of them. And they were just as Max had described: large, black, and monstrous. Translucent, purple-veined wings glistened in the sun's scorching rays as they settled on his body. Like a living, breathing thing.

Solitary Confinement

It is a dark, musty room, gray walls, the plaster ceiling cracked. It is small: ninety-six square feet (I have paced it off). There are no windows and that is what makes it most unbearable—for I can never see the light of day. The only source of illumination is a bare light bulb which hangs suspended from the ceiling. The light it casts is bright white. It hurts my eyes. There is a desk in the room and a bookshelf and a swivel chair. A small cot which serves as my bed occupies one corner.

I do not know why I am here, though I do know I have been here a very long time. Sometimes my mind recalls shadowy images of a life from long ago; images so intimate and real I feel certain I must have lived them: walking alone in the woods on a steamy summer's day; staring up at the clouds as they formed and reformed like a flock of birds heading south; a lover's first kiss; riding my bicycle along empty city streets; playing baseball with my friends in the springtime; walking with my parents to the neighborhood grocery store; my first haircut; being scolded by a shopkeeper for something I did not do; getting knocked to the ground by a cyclist while on the way home from school; hearing my mother shriek in horror when she saw the blood; sleeping in a tent in our backyard, hoping to catch a glimpse of the monsters of gloom as they descended upon our house when the midnight hour approached, monsters I knew existed, though I never was able to see them. Ah! but this is mere nostalgia for a time that never again shall be. Now there is only gray—and this endless monotony.

What am I doing here? I will tell you—though I am certain you will not believe me: I am facing a bookshelf; each of its four shelves contains thirty-one large, black books, with the words "The Book of the Leper, Volume Zed" written in gold on the spine. The books are arranged in ascending order from left to right, beginning with Volumes I, II, and III on the lowest shelf, and ending with Volumes CXXII, CXXIII, and CXXIV on the top shelf. The books themselves are filled with nonsense: collections of every day symbols that taken together have no meaning. Here, for example, are the first two lines of page 365 of The *Book of the Leper*, Volume XIV:

> lvb9tywpeywLdvjbscvu[0tuwepsdvjaspyweporiud ojvhdpgwpfuh
> jdv9erty205208wdvjhafhe08y391t[owrygFJGJEPORG H235Y1]

There is no punctuation; there are no sentences or even words. Simply a random listing of letters, numbers, and punctuation marks. Perhaps it is some code, but I doubt it. Indeed, I spent several weeks pursuing that hypothesis, applying every method of decryption I could think of: rotating the text, breaking it into fragments, rearranging the fragmented parts, folding a page into thirds, fourths, and fifths, then again rotating, fragmenting, and rearranging—but it came to nothing. This is simply gibberish.

I spend my days with a quill pen in hand, copying this strange text onto parchment paper. From eight in the morning until eight at night. There is a pause midday for lunch and again early evening for dinner. Franz, the cell guard, brings my meals. A meal consists of bread, soup, and occasionally, meat. And there is usually broth to drink.

I do not know if you have ever spent time copying nonsense, but it really is quite a laborious undertaking! After only several hours the letters begin to blur and the text itself swims before your eyes. It is increasingly difficult to make a clear and accurate copy. Lunch provides some relief but lasts only a short while. By mid-afternoon your eyes are watering, and your head begins to ache. You wonder if the day will ever come to an end. By the time supper arrives you can hardly think, you gulp down your food without pausing from your work: "a-b-c-d-e-f-g" —> "a-b-c-d-e-f-g". "1-2-3-4-5-6-7" —> "1-2-3-4-5-6-8". Horror! You catch your mistake just as you were turning the page. Of course, now you must start over, redoing the page from the first word to the last. (Not a single mistake will be tolerated. This is what you have been told. You have no choice but to believe it: the penalty is a doubling of the work required each day.) The final hour approaches and you head down the home stretch. Your head is throbbing, sweat pours off your brow. You imagine the horrors they will inflict upon you if you come up short. And even if you manage to produce the required amount, the quality of the copied text will be poor—by now the mistakes must number in the hundreds! You realize the endeavor is hopeless.

Precisely at 8 P.M. the Fraulein (a beautiful German girl; her arrival is the only event I look forward to each day) comes to collect the sheets I have copied. Eleven sheets per day—that is what is required. To miss one's quota—Franz has told me—will result in the most horrid of tortures. (I have never missed my quota, however, so I do not know for sure. This may simply be talk to keep me in line.)

***

"Nonsense is nonsense," I said to myself as the Fraulein left with another day's work. "How long can you keep this up? Day after day for the rest of your life? And what good is it? What purpose does it serve? You get nothing from your labor—only a lousy meal twice a day. What kind of existence is that? Nothing to be proud of, that's for sure!" And what did my captors get from my servitude? On the face of it merely eleven pages each day of nonsensical text. I looked at Franz: a dumb brute, undoubtedly of apish ancestry. Did he know what he was doing here? Did he know what purpose he served? I tried once to strike up a conversation with ol' Franz, to understand his feelings on these matters, but he simply stared at me as if he did not understand my words. And probably he did not, probably he was too stupid to discuss the relative importance of human events. To him it was all nonsense.

And it was then that I realized the full import of my words: Nonsense is nonsense. And since nonsense was nonsense it made sense that any nonsense would suffice. I had no idea what my captors did with the papers I copied, but I couldn't imagine that they actually read them! And so, I resolved to spend the first hour of every day writing down whatever nonsense came into my head—eleven pages worth—and when I was done I would compose a tale of my own choosing: a fantastic, magical tale, filled with color and life. Everything that was denied me here.

***

"What are you doing?" said a female voice. I whirled around and saw the Fraulein not three feet from me! Terror-stricken, I made a vain attempt to hide my story, but she was already moving towards me, her hand outstretched.

"Let me see."

"No," I replied. "It's nothing, really."

She smiled. "You're writing intently, but not from *The Book of the Leper*. Why, it's not even on your desk! What are you up to?"

I said nothing.

"Don't worry," she said and then her voice became a whisper: "I'll tell no one."

"What I do after my work is done is my own affair," I said, although this was misleading: I hadn't even done my work; I'd made up my own nonsense instead of copying theirs.

She laughed. "I promise!"

"Take these." I handed her the eleven pages of nonsense I'd written that morning. "This is what you came for, isn't it?"

The Fraulein took the pages but did not look at them.

"Come now," she said. "Don't be bashful."

I thought the situation over. What was the point of holding out, anyway? All the Fraulein had to do was click her fingers and Franz would be here at once, consigning me to oblivion. I did as she asked.

"It's an excellent story," the Fraulein said as she read my work. "A love story. How I enjoy love stories."

"What are you talking about?" I said. "The story has nothing to do with love. It's about Fortune and Fate."

"No, no, no," she insisted. "I know a love story when I read one, and this is clearly a love story."

"Preposterous!" I cried. "Why, the story contains not a single word about love. It's a story about Fortune and Fate, I say. And I should know—I wrote every word!" Even as the words escaped my lips I realized my fate was sealed.

The Fraulein smiled. "I told you I would tell no one and I shall keep my word: Your secret is safe with me. No one shall know."

Did I dare believe her?

She took me in her arms and led me to the cot. She was stroking my hair. "Let us be honest with each other. Your story is about your love for me."

I opened my mouth to protest, but she brought a finger to my lips, silencing me.

"But what you don't know is that I also want to make

love."

Flabbergasted, I said nothing.

"You are not like the others," she continued. "They do what you tell them, like sheep. You are different: strong, virile, with a mind of your own. Come, let us make love together!" Slowly, deliberately, she began to undo the buttons on her blouse.

"What others?" I said finally. I was trying to put her off, stalling for time so I could figure out what to do.

She laughed. "Why, I believe you're nervous!" She clapped her hands. "But you must not be nervous. You must never be nervous when you make love." From one of her pockets she pulled a vial containing a light-blue liquid. She held it to my lips. "Take this. It will calm you." Looking back, I cannot believe my stupidity, but I drank the vial's contents greedily, as if it was a magic elixir.

Almost at once I felt myself losing consciousness. I tried to fight off the enveloping sleep, but it was no use; the drug was overpowering. As my mind turned to stone, I watched as the Fraulein removed her blouse; her huge German breasts danced before my eyes. *No*, I thought. *You must not let this happen.* My last image was of the Fraulein bending over me, bringing her lips to my lips in an everlasting kiss.

Moments later I was asleep.

***

When I woke the next morning, the Fraulein was gone—and so was my story. "How could you have been so stupid!" I cried. The Fraulein had seduced me, plain and simple. What would happen next was plain and simple, too: she would give my captors my story and I would be shot at dusk.

When Franz came in later that morning with breakfast I was so terrified I could not look into his eyes. But Franz said nothing. He deposited the tray on my desk as usual, then left. *They are going to let you stew*, I thought. They had me where they wanted me: twisting in the wind. Perhaps they would be content to watch me suffer as I fretted over what might happen next. Perhaps so, but probably not. More likely they had horrible tortures in mind, tortures Franz had only hinted at (and then with a shudder) for they were too awful to speak of openly. Needless to say, I had no desire to work that morning. What I really wanted was to tear down those walls and kill every one of my captors I could find, every cell guard, every pretty female informant. But there was nothing I could do to improve my situation—and that was what was hardest to accept. Weeping copiously, torn up inside with the agony of a condemned man, I soon was fast asleep.

I was awakened by the sound of Franz bringing my lunch. I ate ravenously (I had not touched breakfast) and afterwards felt strangely refreshed.

Okay, I thought. *They know what you are up to. And they have already taken from you that which is most precious to you—your work. But this means they can do nothing more to you. As far as they are concerned you are a broken man (though you are not). This means you are free.*

I sat down at my writing desk and pulled from the fourth shelf *The Book of the Leper,* Volume CXXI. I opened it at random, took up my quill pen, plucked a fresh piece of paper from the stack, and wrote across the top in big, bold letters:

EAT FLAMING DEATH FASCIST PIGS

I chuckled. Centered on line one of page one. It was certain to get their attention. It would let them know I knew they knew and did not care. I proceeded to write out the required eleven pages of gibberish. Precisely at 8 P.M. Franz returned.

"Where is the Fraulein?" I asked, feigning naiveté. "Doesn't she always take my work?"

Franz took the pages without saying a word. Then he left.

But later that evening the Fraulein did return. To

play with me, her pet, no doubt. She said not a word as she led me to the bed (as if it were to be my place of execution) and kissed me as she had kissed me the night before. We made love then, as we would make love the next night and the many nights thereafter: mechanically, as if her lovemaking were a drug to mask the suffering caused by my confinement. Or a bribe to silence my wandering pen and ensure obedience to my captors.

***

I dreamed one night of the Fraulein. It was springtime and we were alone on a grassy hill, making love. The air was filled with the sweet scent of honeysuckle. The Fraulein's eyes were closed, and she was smiling. I stroked her skin; it was soft, like silk. She moaned as I caressed her. Her lips beckoned to me and I kissed them. They were moist and red with passion. She rolled onto her back, her hands clutching tufts of grass. "Please," she gasped. "Please." Her voice was light and ethereal, like the voice of a goddess. Our lips met in a passionate kiss. And then she opened herself up to receive me. I thought I would die of happiness at that moment and I felt myself starting to explode.

***

I was awakened by the sound of Franz bringing my breakfast. He did not bother to look at me as he entered the room this time. No doubt he thought I was sleeping off the lovemaking that had been doled out to me the night before. The guard had let down his guard! I, for my part, feigned sleep. Here at last was a chance to escape; who knew when I would get another? One day, certainly, they would tire of this game and would do away with me. I knew what I had to do; the next few moments were critical. I heard the tray clatter as Franz put it on the desk. Then silence. Then the sound of papers being shuffled. Franz was probably looking for more of my stories, but he would find nothing. After several minutes, he scowled, realizing his mission had been in vain. I opened my eyes a fraction of an inch and saw him turn abruptly on his heels and start towards the door.

In a flash I jumped from the bed, picked up the chair, and brought it crashing over his head. He crumpled to the floor without a sound.

"Shouldn't have let down your guard, ol' boy," I said.

I removed his pistol and put it in my belt. Then I went through his pockets. From his right front pocket, I pulled what appeared to be the key to my room. I chuckled. When Franz awoke and began calling for help, the guards would think it was me gone mad! I left the room, locking the door behind me.

I found myself at the end of a long hallway lit by torches that hung suspended from wooden beams which crisscrossed the ceiling. The ceiling itself was low, six feet high at most. The air was musty and oppressive.

I started down the hallway and was amazed to find offices, at ten-foot intervals, on both sides of the hallway, offices laid out exactly like my own. But even more amazing: in each office I saw a man or a woman, hunched over the desk, apparently in intense concentration for I saw not a limb move. I knocked at the open door of one office and, getting no response, walked inside.

A young man was seated at the writing desk. A volume of *The Book of the Leper* lay open before him. I cleared my throat, but he did not respond. *Such devotion to one's work!* I thought. I touched a hard shoulder, I peered into a stony face, lifeless eyes, and a shiver ran up and down my spine: this man was no faithful servant—he had been lapidified. I shuddered realizing that could have been my fate.

I picked up the parchment paper on which the man had been writing. Faithful nonsense to the end. Had he believed what he'd written? Had it given meaning to his life's final moments? I would never know for the man was as good as dead, quite beyond hope. *A stone among stones*, I thought.

I left him then—there was nothing I could do to help

him—and started down the hallway. I discovered other hallways, branching to the left and right, and staircases to other floors. Like my office, none of these places had windows; no views to the outside world. And every ten feet were torches, burning brightly. The offices multiplied, the people in them multiplied, the copies of *The Book of the Leper* multiplied. The prison was a labyrinth of immense proportions.

I took down the nearest torch and held it before me. The flame burned bright and steady. It would do fine. I took a deep breath and said to myself: "here goes."

I walked into an office at random. Another volume of another copy of *The Book of the Leper* lay open on the desk; the parchment paper next to it was half filled out. Seated at the desk was a woman frozen in silence, staring vacantly at the book before her. I, too, had looked into the book, but had seen nothing. What did she see that I did not see? She saw meaning where there was meaninglessness, structure where there was chaos. And she saw those things because she was terrified of facing a meaningless and chaotic world, the world in which she found herself and which had consumed her simply because she had let it.

I set fire to the parchment paper, the opened book, all the other volumes, and then to the cot. Then I left the room.

I repeated this procedure in office after office down hallway after hallway, as I worked my way towards the front entrance. (I knew where the front entrance was, for I had been there once before, when I first passed through its doors; I let Fate carry me back.) I saw flames rising up staircases and shooting out doorways as the fire did its work. And for the first time I heard voices: voices filled with confusion, anger, and despair as my captors realized what was happening. An alarm went off. The voices seemed to draw nearer. I quickened my pace, threw away the torch, and moments later reached the front entrance.

It was unguarded; the entire place was in chaos. I heard cries of "There he is!" and "Shoot him dead!" as I dashed through the front entrance and over a bridge, finding myself on a narrow dirt road on the other side. I ran until I could run no more and then I turned and saw my former prison: it was a gigantic palace, reaching to the sky—and it was engulfed in flames. I stood transfixed by the towering inferno, watched in morbid fascination as red flames licked the sky, and I cried out with joy when a deafening roar went up as the palatial beams crashed to the earth and crumbled into nothingness.

LOVE IN A HIGH-TECH AGE

"Love in a high-tech age is like love in any other age: full of delights, yet fraught with peril."
~William Blythe, speaking to the judge at his divorce proceeding

I committed adultery last night. And today I am a ruined man. Financially ruined, I mean. Morally, too, I suppose, though I don't know that seducing an android is necessarily an immoral act. Regardless of the reasons I invent to explain my actions, my professional reputation has been irreparably harmed. The insidious gossip at the bank—the threats, the innuendo—will spread like wildfire. I would not be surprised if Mr. Dung, our beloved President, makes titillating comments about me at the next meeting of the executive board. But worse than that, worse than the gossip, the jokes, and my certain loss of prestige, is the money I have lost—and the *interest* on that money. But I am getting ahead of myself. Since only by writing *exactly* what happened have I any hope of assuaging my guilt, here I will write, in its entirety, a full and accurate account of events as they occurred, with no literary embellishments or alterations whatsoever.

The android I seduced was named Helen Finch. She appeared at the bank several months ago. Other than myself and several bank officials no one knew Helen's true pedigree. She was the result of a corporate-sponsored research project to produce life-like automatons, the hope being that they would eventually replace bank tellers. Automated teller machines were fine—so the reasoning went—but a true android teller would be far more personal—and profitable. After the initial investment for the machine itself, nothing need ever be spent on salary or benefits. And this third-generation android went far beyond previous versions. Helen was not only capable of performing the functions of a bank teller, she also possessed a *para-synthetic multi-generative personality*; using the latest artificial intelligence techniques based on the application of adaptive resonance theory to artificial neural networks. She was able to modify her personality over time to match changes in her environment, that is, she could adapt to blend in with the personalities of her fellow co-workers whomever they might be. And it went beyond that. Helen was able to modify her synthetic-bio-rhythmic-personality waves to be in harmony with those of a customer, setting up sympathetic vibrations, of an electro-chemical variety, that could, and most likely would, cause the customer to act upon his secret desires. A Mr. Crumb, for example, might come into the bank to make a simple account transfer request and leave having taken out a large new car loan!

Helen was not only personable she was also beautiful. Her blond hair fell to a shapely waist, her blue-eyes twinkled, her complexion was clear, her skin bright and shiny with nary an imperfection. The Helen Model—as we affectionately referred to it—was twenty-two, fresh out of college with a degree in business administration. She was also quite bright with an uncanny memory and the ability to tally large sums without the aid of a calculating device. We did have one concern, however, and thus the reason for her clandestine introduction to the bank: would an android such as Helen be *too* perfect and end up engendering suspicion and mistrust amongst the employees? If so, that would have meant colossal failure, for the goal of the project was precisely the opposite! In any event, our worries proved unfounded. No one suspected anything was amiss, and I remember patting Mr. Dung on the back when Helen's initial three-month trial period had ended.

It was September 8, 2030. The date is etched in my memory. I left my home after dinner, around 7 P.M. The sky was filled with thick, dark thunderclouds and to the south I thought I heard the rumble of thunder. The forecast had been for clear skies and I remember thinking this weather was somehow strange. (It was one of those moments that stick in your mind—you have no idea why.) *It is going to storm*, I thought. I had some work to do in preparation for a meeting with Dr. Josh Friedman the next morning. Dr. Friedman was applying for a loan of fifty million dollars; renovations were planned for his department store chain. I had first met Dr. Friedman the day he applied for the loan. Over my secretary's objection he had rushed into my office demanding to talk to the Vice-President of Loan Services directly. An affable man, mid-forties, jolly face, bright-red hair, rather large around the middle, he explained that his department store chain had fallen on hard times, having been upstaged by the young and dynamic Pizzazo's for Women department store chain, the department stores "with pizzazz!" I nodded sympathetically and told him I'd see what I could do. He clasped my hand warmly. "I knew I could count on you," he said. "I knew it! Midwest Services is indeed the 'bank that cares.'"

"But I make no promises," I cautioned.

"A fair consideration of my plight is all I ask." He shook my hand again and then was gone. That conversation had occurred several months before. Unfortunately, I had been delinquent in getting to his application. To tell the truth, I had lost it, or rather misplaced it under a stack of papers on my desk.

But now I was of necessity concentrating on the Friedman matter. Dr. Friedman himself was to return to the bank the next day. From the letter he had sent I gathered he was quite upset. And he had reason to be. Midwest Services guaranteed a two-week waiting period, no longer, on all loans. Dr. Friedman had been waiting over three months. I had extricated myself from situations far worse than this in the past and would simply have to invent a plausible explanation for the delay. But things were even stickier than that: Dr. Friedman (I had learned) was a close acquaintance of Mr. Dung. If he suspected I was playing games with his application and conveyed his suspicions to Mr. Dung, I would be quickly dismissed. Mr. Dung had never liked me. At least not since the time (this was many years ago) when we had gotten drunk together and ended up in a place of questionable repute. It was all innocent and inconsequential, but the damage was done. (You see, Mr. Dung was married at the time. His wife left him shortly thereafter.)

Helen was standing near a desk in the front lobby when I entered, wearing a lacy, white blouse and a bright red skirt with bold black buttons down one side. "Hello Mr. Blythe," she said. "What brings you in this evening?"

Helen had been at Midwest Services over three months and—I suddenly realized—this was the first conversation I'd ever had with her. The android certainly did look life-like and, in all honesty, rather sexy. If one hadn't known better, one would have sworn she was human. She was fidgeting with a paperweight she'd

picked up from the desk—an android would never fidget!
—her smile was warm and infectious, and her blue eyes
were filled with naïveté. And this was where things got,
shall we say, uncomfortable. Now I realized it could never
have been the case, but she looked exactly like a woman
I had been thinking about earlier that evening. The
blouse. The skirt. The cheerful disposition. The aura of
mystery that seemed to hang over her. *A remarkable job
of engineering*, I thought.

"Work to do," I said in reply. "And you?"

"The same. But remember the more one works the
more work one gets to do. That's Helen's Maxim." She
smiled and tossed her blond hair over her shoulders. A
nice feminine touch. "But when you've bills to pay, and
mouths to feed, I guess there's not much else you can
do."

"I didn't know you had children," I said feigning
surprise.

"I don't," she replied. "I've never met the right man."
She winked. "No, I'm speaking of my cats: Happy, Lucky,
and Dopey. They've appetites as voracious as any
child's."

"I know what you mean," I said. "Our kids are eating
us out of house and home."

She laughed. "Kids, cats—they're all the same."

There was something about Helen's voice that
bothered me. An ethereal flutter in the intonation of her
words, an enchanting modularity. In the bits and pieces
of conversation I'd overheard she'd always seemed, well,
completely professional. Why would she alter her speech
patterns now? I had to admit I found this modulation in
her voice both different and exciting. I couldn't put my
finger on it, but it was almost as if it were meant *for me*.

"Well, I can't stand around talking all night," I said
and added jokingly, "even if I'd like to."

"Me, too," she replied. "See you later."

Seated at my desk, I opened Dr. Friedman's folder.
His credentials were impeccable: Past President of the
American Association of Retailers, founder of Friedman's
Department Stores, a chain of twenty-six department

stores in the Southeastern United States, board member of the Baton Rouge, Louisiana Board of Education, leader of the Boy Scout's Troop 513, a churchgoer (Baton Rouge United Baptist Church). Married twenty-two years, four children (two boys, two girls). Hobbies: camping, fishing, motor boating.

I didn't know what I could do for Dr. Friedman. He wanted money—but, then, everyone wanted money. At least that was the way it seemed. Economic times were hard; the country was on the verge of recession. In cases such as this one (and there were many such cases) it always came down to a simple question: why should X get the bank's money instead of Y? What had X done that Y had failed to do? In this case, X (Dr. Friedman) had done nothing to improve his stature. X had been content to rely on past successes for future revenues; X had refused to modernize; X had refused to explore new marketing methods. In fact, it was X's competitors Y, Y', and Y'' who had been innovative, who together constituted the real reason behind X's decline. Best to wait for them to apply for loans and give the bank's money to them!

"Mr. Blythe."

I looked up. Helen was at the door.

"Yes."

"I want you."

Now, what exactly did Helen mean by that phrase? Based on my previous reflections, I took it to mean: "I want to be involved with you romantically." The results of which I shall presently relate. But undoubtedly, I was mistaken. Certainly, she simply meant: "I want you to do something for me—for the bank. I want you to perform a non-romantic function." Indeed, that is what her programming would have required of her. And as I look back at events I shudder at my impertinence. How could I have jumped to such a conclusion? Was it Helen's overpowering air of femininity—coldly designed and calmly implemented—that led my mind astray? Was it her perfectly sculpted body: a body no human male could possibly resist? Or was it my own moral failings that, confronted by such an entity, inevitably led to my ruin?

"Come in," I said, after a long pause. I was cogitating not on the meaning of the phrase, "I want you," but on my future course of action. Did I want her in the manner she wanted me? I most certainly did (to deny it would have been an act of self-deception), but I had a lovely wife and two charming daughters and—

"Mr. Blythe."

My palms were beginning to sweat, my heart to palpitate. There is only so much a man can take after all! And as the fog of temptation began to settle upon me I found myself succumbing. What can I say? I knew what I was about to do was not only wrong it was downright foolish, that it would lead me into a swamp of misery where an overpowering miasma would certainly mean my doom. Undoubtedly because of this my brain was hard at work pondering the consequences. With my attentions focused elsewhere, what might this mean for my (proper) work at the bank? What might this mean for Dr. Friedman? What might this mean for the future of his department store chain? And what would *that* mean for his customers? These were the questions that filtered (quickly) through my mind as I stared at Helen's incredible figure, her bombshell bust and tight derriere. Alas, it was to no avail.

Helen entered and closed the door behind her.

"You look beautiful tonight," I said, "but, then, you always look beautiful."

She smiled and looked at the floor. "Mr. Blythe, I . . ."

"And I know why you are here."

"You do?"

"It would seem you cannot resist me."

"Mr. Blythe, I think I should tell you something."

"And I cannot resist you, Helen. When I look into your eyes—they are all a-glow—I tremble all over. My thoughts wander where they should not go . . ."

"I'm an android."

I laughed. "And so are we all. Tin-plated robots. Finely-tuned automatons. Sophisticated Turing machines.

Logical byproducts of a cold and unfeeling universe."

"No," she continued. "I mean it. I'm nothing but a sophisticated thinking machine. I was constructed in a research lab in Oak Ridge, Tennessee. My nanocircuits were finely tuned to mimic human neural circuitry. My programming directs me to perform as a human being." She laughed. "Don't you see? I've been flirting. And isn't that exactly what you wanted me to do?"

"It matters naught."

And, so saying, I gathered her into my arms and kissed her lips. She did not resist. At the time her acquiescence did not surprise me—by this time I imagined myself a true Casanova—but later, after events had reached their dreadful conclusion, I wondered why—why had Helen not resisted me? After all, this was not part of her programming! But on further reflection I realized Helen was doing exactly what she had been designed to do: adapt her personality to the situation in which she found herself. Fit in and please her human masters.

"Yes," Helen said finally, showering me with kisses and running her fingers through my silvering hair, "You are kind, a very sweet man."

I felt myself blushing as she whispered softly into my ear, "Shall we?"

"Not so fast, my dear," I replied suavely. "In love as in finance, patience leads to a higher rate of return!"

"Oh," she sighed. "You are a witty man. Manly and witty. A witty, manly man."

Our lips crushed together in a passionate kiss and we fell to the floor.

Just then the fax machine (of all things) started printing noisily in the far side of my office. "Just a minute," I said and extending a long arm I plucked off the emerging piece of paper. "STOCK CRASH" it began, but I tossed it aside. "Not important," I said, half to Helen and half to the bank. "Tonight, nothing is as important as our love!"

STOCK CRASH PANICS FINANCIAL WORLD

NEW YORK — News of the collapse of Dr. Josh Friedman's retail empire has been met with horror on Wall Street. Unbeknownst to the banking community, Dr. Friedman had managed to gain control of forty percent of the silver market, fifty-four percent of the cotton market, and ninety-two percent of the market in pork bellies. He has recently sold off his assets in all three commodities, at ridiculously low prices, to pay back a half-dozen loans that have come due on his entrepreneurial dealings, most notably those involving the Friedman's Department Store chain. The silver market has taken a nose dive; the cotton and pork belly markets are in shambles—even the stock market has been affected, down over five hundred points since the opening bell.

The President of the New York Stock Exchange took to the floor at two o'clock this afternoon in an attempt to shut down the exchange and prevent any further market erosion. But his shouts were inaudible over the din of several hundred stockbrokers all frantically issuing orders to sell. Apparently, the man could not even be seen, for the air was a blizzard of white tickets, each another order to bail out.

Computerized stock trading has begun, sending the market into a tailspin. At this very hour computers all over the country are coming to life . . .

. . . even William Blythe's new state-of-the-art FSX Model 5000 voice-activated computer, the article may well have continued, for that is what happened. Of course, I knew none of this at the time: I was being consumed by and was myself consuming the delectable Helen of Troy. If only that night could have lasted forever! If only I had never come to realize the reality of my plight! FSX. What a wonderful machine! It was one of the first fifth-generation voice-controlled computers to come out of Tru-Blu Thinking Machines Corporation. With a sleek titanium-alloy body, blue LED lights, elegant meshed front panels, and gently-purring disk drives, it was a real beauty. And like Helen it was intelligent. Using a complex set of heuristic algorithms based on the latest neuro-psychological studies from Stockholm, Sweden, FSX was able to synchronize itself with a user's behavior, and by doing so was able to suggest alternatives (whatever the scenario) based on the wishes and desires of the user. The similarity to the android was uncanny. And between the two of them, well, I didn't have a chance.

I remembered trembling with anticipation as I unpacked the box, pulled out FSX's console, CPU, and disk drives. It assembled in a flash, was up and running without a hitch, and responding smoothly to my every command. FSX meant wonders for my work: for the first time I was freed from the confines of my desk. I would strut about my office issuing orders: Buy this stock! Sell that one! Process this request! Reject that one! All the while peering out the window of my office at Mr. Lakewood's secretary, Ms. Eaten, at her slim figure and wonderfully shaped legs. (Mr. Lakewood was Director of Capital Acquisitions; he'd held the position for as long as anyone could remember. A lifeless creature, I had never liked him.) Ms. Eaten had seen me once, had smiled and winked. A gesture I took as an invitation, though I had never taken the matter further.

As I sit here at my writing desk, penning this sad and woeful tale, it dawns on me: Perhaps that wink was not a wink but an expression of disbelief? Perhaps Ms. Eaten had warned Helen of my impertinence? Perhaps last night's episode was a clever ploy designed by Ms. Eaten to bring ruin upon me? Nor could I forget Mr. Lakewood, Mr. Dung, and Dr. Friedman. All had reasons to wish my downfall: Mr. Lakewood for my peeping at his secretary, Mr. Dung for past wrongs he felt I had committed, Dr. Friedman for my refusal to grant him the loan he so desperately needed; all were stodgy old men at heart, not the type to appreciate my boyish antics. It could have been any of them; it could have been any one of several others. But though it was possible it was also unlikely for none of these people seemed capable of such a sinister ploy. The following conversation—a most unwished for climax to our encounter—is of necessity a reconstruction but must represent what occurred that night. I heard only Helen's voice, I saw only Helen. As for the rest, well, it was technology at its finest hour—even if it was to mean my demise.

Helen: "Do you love me?"

FSX: "Five-thousand shares of Technology Limited. Sell?"

Me: "Yes!"

Helen: "Will you love me forever?"

FSX: "Six-thousand shares of United Intermediary Services. Sell?"

Me: "Yes! Yes!"

Helen: "I am yours."

FSX: "Fifty-thousand shares of Networking International. Sell?"

"One-hundred-thousand shares of Union Enterprises. Sell?"

"Five-hundred thousand shares of Midwest Services Incorporated. Sell?"

Me: "Yes! Yes! Yes! Yes!"

While I was drowning in romantic bliss, my lovely computer was busy liquidating the remainder of my assets! I finished the night a satisfied lover—and in total financial ruin. House, cars, wife, all is lost. Today I must begin atonement for my sins. I will see to it that Helen is dismissed immediately, of course. And then I will return to the business at hand, to Dr. Friedman, and to other financial matters. And I will deny any involvement with the sudden departure of Helen Finch.

The Roses of Charon

The doorbell rang. Meredith Clark was in the kitchen preparing lunch. She turned off the burner under the frying pan and went to answer.

"Hello," said the middle-aged man who greeted her. "My name is Frederick White the Third. You do not know me, but I have something here"—he pointed to a small cardboard box which he had set down on the porch—"that will make you rich beyond your wildest dreams." The man was dressed in a dark suit, tie, and black shoes which were scuffed. His oily, black hair was slicked back, and beads of perspiration clung to his brow. Steel-rimmed glasses perched atop the bridge of a bulbous nose. Standing no more than five feet six, and weighing much more than he probably desired, he was short and fat. A short, fat man.

Meredith's first impulse was to wish Frederick White a good day, then shut the door. These salesmen really were becoming a nuisance! But something about the man intrigued her. Without realizing what she was doing, she found herself inviting him inside. He entered with a smile, bowing as he did so.

He sat down on the sofa and crossed his legs. Then he pulled off his glasses, pulled out a handkerchief, and began rubbing the lenses. "As I was saying. My name is Frederick White the Third. My father—whom I never knew—was Frederick White the Second. His father—my grandfather—who taught my father this secret of eternal wealth—was Frederick White the First, though that was not his real name. His real name was Joseph Park and if neither name means anything to you do not worry. My grandfather was a shy man and felt that if his name came to be associated with this treasure, he'd never get a moment's rest—fame in a day, it would have been. And he wanted none of that. Do you see?"

Meredith had to suppress a chuckle. Frederick White certainly was bizarre! He reminded her of a figure from her past, but she couldn't put her finger on who it was. That eccentric art teacher from first grade, perhaps. The one who imagined he was a descendent of Vincent Van Gogh. Or that boisterous singer in the church choir, the one who later ran off with the pastor's wife.

Meredith was conscious of Frederick White's hand on her dress, gently rubbing the cloth. "This is remarkable material," he said, his voice soft and velvety. "Where was this purchased?"

"Hillman's department store," she answered. "Though I don't see what's so special about it. It's a simple cotton dress. What do you find so intriguing?"

"No, it's not the material. It's the pattern of the dress that interests me. See how the circles grow progressively smaller from the front of the dress to the back? And these three lines weave back and forth but intersect only at the waist; there two of the three cross. Isn't that amazing?"

"Sir, this dress is solid blue. There are no lines or circles or any shapes on it!"

"Ah, then maybe it isn't the dress, maybe it's something else. Well, no matter." Frederick White jumped up and clapped his hands. "Hi, ho! Hi, ho!" he cried, and he burst out laughing. "Have a look at this!" And from the box he pulled a ruby. To call it majestic would have been an understatement: it was the size of a walnut, by far the largest jewel Meredith had ever seen. "Where in heaven did you get such a stone?" she asked.

"It was belched from within the mighty depths of Charon," he replied with a mischievous grin. "A planet in the farthest reaches of the galaxy." He paused. "Would you like it?"

"What woman wouldn't kill for such a treasure?"

Frederick White smiled. "The ruby is yours, my dear. If only you do as I ask. One small favor, nothing more."

She tensed. "And what might that be?"

"Only the smallest of favors; practically inconsequential. A mere trifle, I assure you." He smiled once again and said, "I would like you to give me that dress."

Meredith drew back as if a burning sun had touched her. "My husband gave me this dress. On our first anniversary. It *is* plain. But it is very special. Surely there is something else."

"Come now. With this ruby you could buy a thousand dresses. And much more, besides."

"No, there must be something else I could give you. If it's the material of the dress that interests you—or the color of the cloth—I have others that would surely satisfy. Come, I will show you." She started towards the bedroom, but Frederick White would have none of it.

"The reason why is of no concern to you!" he cried, his face red with indignation. "The ruby for the dress; that is my proposition." He had drawn close to her again, and again was fingering the dress, caressing the material with his left hand, while his right held the ruby, which he waved before her eyes.

"I think you'd better go," she said. "Your stone is probably nothing but a fake."

Frederick White's eyes opened wide. "How dare you make such an insinuation! I have half a mind to—" He glowered, and the veins stood out on his neck. For one frightening moment she thought he might strike her, but then he sighed and put his hands in his pockets. His eyes looked like two black circles on his pudgy round face. "I see that you drive a hard bargain, Mrs. Clark," he said. "Well, then—if I must, I must!"

***

When Meredith awoke she was lying on her bed. Her head ached. She looked at the clock on the nightstand and saw that it was five in the afternoon. She went into the kitchen and poured herself a lemonade. The late afternoon sun was streaming through the window over the sink; it reflected off the azure wallpaper, casting a blue haze throughout the room. Five o'clock! Where had the time gone? She had so much to do and she hadn't even started. The chocolate cake—Tom's favorite— needed at least an hour. What had he wanted for dinner? Roasted butternut squash, yes, and pear soup. But that required a trip to the market.

She thought she heard a car pulling into the driveway and she went to the back door. But the driveway was empty. That was odd. She was certain she had heard a sound. And Tom should be arriving at any moment. She opened the door and went outside into the shimmering heat. She saw the sun beginning its descent in a violet sky. The sunsets were spectacular this time of year. She and her husband had planned a trip to Kregor Lake later to observe one. It would be a romantic occasion. Because of the demands of Tom's job at the research lab, they had little time together these days. He kept saying it would get better, but she was beginning to wonder if that time would ever come.

Meredith looked up and down the silent street. She saw a sprinkler hard at work in a neighbor's lawn, but her neighbors were nowhere to be seen. She saw lifeless pines. Withered shrubbery. The cracked ground. It hadn't rained in weeks.

She sighed. She loved Tom more than he would ever know. More than he was worthy of, he told her one evening as they walked arm-in-arm through Daphne

Park. But today was his forty-fifth birthday and she wanted to make it special for him.

It was then that Meredith realized she was wearing her pink nightgown. And that was odd for she had no recollection of having taken off the dress. At first, she wasn't concerned. She'd been prone to periods of absentmindedness for years. She'd even mentioned it to her doctor. It was quite normal, he told her. The advancement of the years.

Meredith went back inside and saw an empty cardboard box on the cherry end table in the living room. No, it wasn't empty. The bottom was lined with dirt embedded with chunks of coal. And suddenly she remembered what had happened.

She put down her glass, a cold sweat breaking out across her brow. She looked in the bedroom. She looked in the closets. She looked in the master bath. The gates of hell were about to open and swallow her whole, for the dress was gone and Tom would be beside himself at the loss of such a precious gift. Her eyes filled with tears as she recalled Frederick White's exaggerated smile. His incessant demands. His unwanted touch. She wanted someone to tell her that she had been dreaming. Or that she was dreaming now.

"God help me," she mumbled. Tom would never believe her. He would suspect an impropriety for sure. Lately, every look, every conversation with another man—however innocent—required an explanation. She feared sometimes that he would strike her, though he never had. He didn't mean to be like that, of course. Even though he often was. It was his job, those sixteen-hour days. Tom was an engineer at NASA's Langley, Virginia facility. Meredith didn't understand what he did, exactly—it had something to do with developing new methods of space travel—but she knew it was stressful. Many days he felt as if it was tearing him apart.

She heard Tom's car pulling into the driveway. The sound of his heels on the pavement and up the granite steps. Watched in terror as the front door opened with a maddening slowness. What was she to do? And it was then that she smelled the wild roses and tears welled up in her eyes.

The truth, Meredith, she thought to herself, *you must tell the truth.*

***

Two weeks later, the letter arrived. It was a simple extortion letter, just as Tom had said it would be, and she took it straight to the police. They received it with a nonchalant air. "Oh, we know all about this guy," she was told. "He's wanted in a dozen states."

The letter, which was unsigned, stated things plainly: she was to put one thousand dollars in an envelope and place it behind one of the rose bushes that surrounded the statue of Governor Augustus in Daphne Park. She was to do this the following evening at 8 P.M. If she complied, the dress would be returned. If she did not, the dress would be burned.

Sergeant Burns saw them that very afternoon. A tall, lanky man with stark red hair and penetrating eyes, he was sitting in a soft leather chair with a meerschaum pipe between his lips. They had no time to lose, he said. This man was a slippery character. He had half a dozen aliases and was a master of disguise, but the outcome for his victims was always the same: a bullet through the head.

Meredith shuddered. Tom took her hands in his, looked into her eyes, and smiled. He was looking at her as if she was a wallflower, she thought.

"Now, this is what we want you to do," the sergeant continued, pointing a long, bony finger at Meredith. He opened the desk drawer and took out a white business envelope. "This contains what the gentleman asked for. You are to do as instructed. We will keep the park under twenty-four-hour surveillance. When he comes to retrieve the envelope—bam!—we nab him." Sergeant Burns clapped his hands for effect. "It's quite simple, really."

"And if something goes wrong?" It was Tom. "Not that you haven't taken into account every contingency,

Sergeant, but even the best laid plans have been known to go awry. As I'm sure you'd be first to admit."

"Why, no, nothing will go wrong." Sergeant Burns smiled. "We'll post an officer at your house, as well, of course. Twenty-four-hour duty."

Meredith took the envelope. "Anything else?"

"Well . . . yes, there is one other thing. We know from the gentleman's past behavior that he has a penchant for young women wearing blue dresses. Pretty, young women. If you know what I mean. We can only surmise that he saw you clothed in such a garment. Do you remember an incident in the preceding days or even months? Something—however odd—that may have stuck in your memory?"

Meredith looked puzzled. "I don't know. I was wearing the dress the day he came to see me, but I hadn't worn it . . . why, in years."

"You're quite certain."

"Yes."

"No." It was Tom and he looked positively angry, his green eyes glowing in the pale light of the room. "What are you talking about? You've worn that dress on many occasions." He addressed the sergeant. "On our last anniversary we were at the theater. I recall it clearly: a man meeting White's description came up to Meredith, claiming to know her, though she insisted she'd never seen him before. He left without a word at my insistence. Still—it was many months ago—I can't see how—"

"Mr. White is known to—shall we say—take his time with his victims."

Meredith shuddered. "Please," she said, "We can replace the dress. It doesn't matter."

Ah, Tom continued, rising from his chair, and pacing nervously across the room. But it *did* matter. He'd read about these attacks in the papers. The man was a pervert. He must be stopped at any cost. And he would be. For, like all criminals, he had gone too far. This matter of the dress. A serious mistake. The sergeant was to correct him if he was wrong—but for the first time Mr. White had allowed one of his victims to converse with him *before* the fatal attack. Why? What was he after? This business about the ruby—had the sergeant considered it fully? Perhaps the clue to the entire affair. According to Meredith, it was quite a gem. Where had White obtained it? And why would he offer to exchange it for a simple piece of fabric? Whatever the man's motive, his actions on this occasion would lead to his downfall. The police would be there to arrest him when he hurried across Daphne Park in the wild light of an enchanted evening, thrust his greedy fingers into a rose bush that contained, not that which he sought, but thorns. Touché!

Tom looked at Meredith and smiled, and it was then she realized she no longer knew who he was.

"Yes," she said to Sergeant Burns. "This is what we must do."

***

The doorbell rang. Meredith knew who was there—who it had to be—but she opened the door anyway. It was as if Fate was pulling her ahead. And when she saw the pallid face, the thin lips, the monstrous eyes, it was all she could do to remain calm.

"May I come in?"

It was mid-afternoon, the heat pouring down out of the sky. She was alone. Her husband would not be home for several hours. And the police were patiently waiting in a park on the other side of town.

"I did as you asked." The color rising slowly into her cheeks.

"Of course."

She looked past him, her eyes straining to catch a glimpse of the guard outside, but she saw no-one, heard only a dog barking angrily on the corner.

"It was nothing." He clicked his fingers.

She noticed that he was carrying a large hat box. And she knew what it contained. She imagined the cold steel, the molten lead. He was like a man in a dream, but unlike in a dream he could not be denied. She looked at him closely, trying to read his thoughts, which she knew, his intentions, which she knew as well but did not understand. Then she looked past him, at the pink houses, the matchstick pines, the cumulus clouds dotting the sky. She saw the sun overhead, its rays beating down upon the earth.

On the sofa in the living room, she asked what he had come for.

He smiled. She'd been most punctual, following his directions to the letter. And yet—there was one other thing.

The liquid sound of his voice. Those eyes that seemed to draw her in. He went over to the living room window and shut the crimson curtains. He turned the lamp down low.

She heard the asthmatic gasp of a car motor and for a moment she thought it might be Tom arriving early—perhaps he'd had a premonition something was wrong—but the sound faded away, as if to seal her fate. She closed her eyes and sighed, hands clenched, knuckles white.

She was wearing gray slacks and a light-yellow blouse. Her long, auburn hair pulled back off her shoulders. She was beautiful, he said. He reached out to touch her. Meredith felt as if she was about to swoon. This could not be happening, she thought. Not to her.

"Shoot me if that's what you intend," she said. "But I'll not betray my husband." Her eyes were cold and lifeless.

He took the lid off the hat box. It would be a small, silver gun, she thought, with a highly polished barrel. A single bullet in the chamber. A bullet that was meant for her.

"Aha!" he cried.

Meredith could not suppress a cry when he took from the box not the instrument of her death, but a dress—her dark-blue, cotton dress—and a dozen red roses which he put in a vase that had materialized out of nowhere.

"They are so beautiful!" she gasped. The flowers were the deepest darkest red she had ever seen. And they had an intoxicating aroma.

"Put it on, please," Frederick White implored her, the dress cradled in his arms. His black eyes danced in the dying light of the room.

Her heart was pounding as she acquiesced. He gazed at her lovingly while he delivered a lecture about the Infinite Nature of Time and Space. "Time itself is endless," he said, "but your time on the earth is not. The space you will occupy during your visit here is a mere stitch in the fabric of the cosmos. This you must always remember."

The heavenly aroma of wild roses settled over the room, a honeyed scent that threatened to suffocate her until she was forced to cry out, "Stop! Please!"

Frederick White drew back as if he'd been touched by a white-hot flame. He looked like a ghostlike silhouette, with the air of a devil swirling about him. It was then that Meredith realized he didn't look anything at all like the man she had remembered him to be. *That* Frederick White was short and fat. *This* Frederick White was something else. Something else entirely.

"Yes," he said in a wispy, insomniac voice. "I guess my time is up."

And suddenly Meredith was no longer afraid. She was emboldened. She brought herself up to her full height, her arms akimbo. "You're no murderer, Mr. White," she said. "Nor are you an extortionist. You're a coward and it's I who have been deceived. Now, tell me who you really are."

Frederick White brought a stubby finger to his chin and eyed Meredith up and down as if deciding what to do or say, if anything. Finally, he spoke: "The truth, then, since you insist. I'm from the planet Charon. I was sent here to study your planet's civilization. Its customs and conventions. Your integrity is most admirable, but I have yet to pass judgment on the rest of your world." He pulled himself up proudly, a beatific expression upon his face.

Meredith was a practical woman and she didn't believe Frederick White's words for a moment, but it was obvious he believed them and—

"I see." She smiled.

He picked up the empty box and started towards the door. "Good-bye, my dear. I'll bother you no more."

His words trailed off as he shuffled out the door, hanging suspended in the air for as long as the dust of that great comet which will never return hangs suspended in space.

At dinner that evening Meredith told Tom what had happened. The police were no longer needed, she said. The ransom had not been taken. The dress was hers once more. "Frederick White certainly was a most eccentric man," she concluded, speaking to herself now for her husband didn't seem to be listening. "The world is full of the strangest people!"

A Journey Through the Wormhole

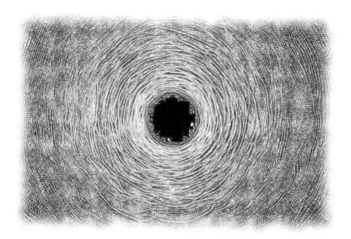

❝It will work," the scientist said as he stroked his full, black beard and gazed lovingly at the silvery apparatus. "It must."

He was speaking to the chief science reporter for the Los Angeles Times, a short stocky man of about thirty-five with bushy black hair, dark eyes, and a slightly rounded chin. The reporter was scribbling the scientist's every word onto a manila writing pad. When dealing with a once in a lifetime story, you do not miss a thought.

"The object to be sent through is placed over there," the scientist said, pointing to a portal adjacent to the apparatus.

The reporter was facing an immense structure perhaps thirty feet wide by twenty feet high by ten feet deep. It was constructed almost entirely out of clear, thin tubules through which a silvery liquid was circulating at a slow but constant speed. In the middle of the structure were two steel pillars that stretched nearly to the ceiling, a good forty feet. They were connected to each other by a third, and much smaller, metal beam. The pillars, the reporter learned, were actually hollow and contained the sophisticated electronics that controlled the apparatus. Mounted on one of the pillars was a large video screen, now blank. On the adjacent pillar was an analogue clock with black numerals and red hands that were steadily moving.

The pillars performed two functions. First, they provided the propulsive force to circulate the silvery liquid through the tubules, a liquid which was used to keep the entire apparatus at a constant—and very cold—temperature. Second, when a switch was pressed, the electrical potential of two previously-generated proton beams was increased to seven tera-electron volts.

The proton beams traveled through an adjacent set of much smaller tubules until they converged, from opposite directions, onto a chamber, resulting in the excitation of the chamber's atoms to high energy levels. After a sufficient period of time, the electric potential of the chamber also reached seven tera-electron volts at which point it would vanish, having been sent on its way.

Once again, the scientist indicated the portal to the left of the apparatus—the reporter had merely glanced at it before—which, he said, led to the chamber.

The portal was a square-framed structure, perhaps five feet high and four feet wide. It was sculpted out of a highly-polished black stone-like material that resembled onyx and was striated with alternating white and silver bands. It seemed to sparkle under the bright lights of the laboratory.

"Fascinating," the reporter said. He went over to the portal and—without thinking—placed his hand on the structure. The material was cold, so cold, in fact, that it seemed to burn his skin. With a howl, he quickly pulled his hand away.

The scientist chuckled. "Careful," he said. "The chamber must be kept at constant minus twenty-six degrees Celsius. The material that encloses the chamber is far colder. Cold enough to cause irreparable damage to human skin tissue after even brief exposure."

"And what have you sent through?" the reporter asked.

"A variety of objects," the scientist said. "A small rubber ball, a mahogany rocking chair, a potted plant, and a blue parrot. All survived. After arriving at its destination, the parrot flew away and was never seen again." He paused. "Now it's time to send something bigger."

The reporter observed that the portal looked to be just big enough to admit a man. Prodded by the scientist, he stuck his head inside. The inner surface of the chamber was made of an exotic-looking material: "cryogenic thermo-insulation," the scientist had explained, "to protect against the cold." The air within was rarefied and pure, like the air atop a mountain peak (the reporter had had a similar sensation when embedded in a scientific exhibition that scaled Mount Tupungato in South America) and after a moment he began to feel lightheaded. And then—he was not sure how it happened—he found himself fully within the chamber. He had collapsed into what seemed to be a plush armchair.

It was dark. So dark, in fact, that it almost seemed invisible. The reporter had never been one to feel claustrophobic. He had spent six months in a submarine, once, reporting on the psychological effects of long-term submersion. But this was something else entirely. The existence of nothingness. The horror of negation. The reporter felt frozen in place, unable to move, unable to think, held hostage by an unseen force that made him stare into a black abyss. He was inside only for a few moments, mind you, only the briefest period of time, but it was long enough. He had never felt such terror. A moment longer, he knew, and he surely would have screamed.

"Ahoy!" It was the scientist calling, bringing the reporter out of his reverie. The reporter was shaking uncontrollably and felt dizzy as if the chamber had been sent spinning on a mad voyage to nowhere.

"This button is the key," the scientist continued when the reporter withdrew, still trembling. His left index finger caressed a large red button on the side of the device. "Press it and you start—or stop—the operation."

"Shooting beams of photons through a wormhole is one thing," the reporter said. "But a man?"

They were talking about Wormhole #38, or, the "Wormhole to the Stars" as it had been dubbed in the press. And the apparatus—which had taken years to construct—was a wormhole generator.

"It's not difficult to generate a wormhole," the scientist continued. "What is challenging is finding a way to keep it from collapsing. It does not represent a natural state. And nature abhors unnatural states."

"Of course."

Once merely theoretical constructs, wormholes had fascinated physicists for decades. They should have been possible—nothing in physics forbade them—yet no one had been able to solve the complicated equations that would enable their creation. Until now.

It had started as a scientific challenge by a group of wealthy industrialists: create and maintain a wormhole, transport a human being a distance of at least ten light-years, return him safely to Earth, and write it up for publication in a peer-reviewed journal. The last requirement was to ensure, one, that the journey was not a hoax, and, two, that the relativistic effects of the journey were overcome (i.e., that the celestial traveler returned within his lifetime, making the process practical). A prize of ten million dollars awaited the winner. The challenge would expire after the first successful journey or at the end of ten years, whichever came first. To date, no one had made the attempt. Nine years had elapsed.

"According to Einstein's theory of relativity," the scientist said, "energy curves spacetime. On extremely small scales—on the order of Planck's constant—the curvature is so immense it gives rise to what is known as quantum foam. The foam in turn gives rise to microscopic wormholes which can be harnessed to create what is termed a wormhole bridge.

"Now, the bridge must be kept at a constant temperature of minus two hundred seventy-three degrees Celsius or approximately absolute zero. At that temperature time essentially stops, making faster-than-light travel possible." The scientist smiled. "And that, if I do say so myself, was my great insight. Others did not realize that temperature is the key."

"How can a man live in such an environment?" the reporter asked.

"The temperature inside the chamber is kept at constant negative twenty-six degrees Celsius. That is uncomfortable for a human, but livable."

"And how do you prevent the temperature of the chamber from adversely affecting the temperature of the wormhole? It would seem that might upset the delicate balance of the entire apparatus."

"You are right to be concerned," the scientist replied. "The temperature of the chamber is far greater than that of the wormhole. The wormhole should evaporate under such conditions. But it won't. You see, the chamber is surrounded by a material that is exactly three degrees above absolute zero. A second layer of material—the cryogenic layer—provides further insulation, allowing the chamber to have its own internal temperature, which, as I said, is minus twenty-six degrees Celsius."

"Remarkable." The reporter was indeed impressed. "However," he continued after a moment's reflection, "it would seem to me that by accelerating the chamber you are creating heat which might wreak havoc with the wormhole. I keep coming back to that point, but it does seem crucial."

"Your questions are probing," the scientist said with obvious admiration. "I see why you are highly regarded in your field." He smiled and patted the wormhole-generating machine. "This is what makes it possible," he said. "This marvelous machine. Think of it this way: what happens to a bullet in a gun when the trigger is pulled?"

"Why, it is hurled outwards by the explosion of the

powder and accelerated through the air."

"Generating heat. In an analogous way, this device provides the propulsive force to accelerate the contents of the chamber through the wormhole, which also generates heat. One might think that this acceleration, which approaches the speed of light, would result in a near infinite increase in temperature which would result in the disintegration of the wormhole. But that does not happen.

"This machine siphons off the created energy through a process called backwash. It is complicated, but the underlying theory is fairly simple. Because of conservation of mass-energy around each endpoint of the wormhole—what is termed a wormhole mouth—the increase in energy as the chamber is accelerated results in forward momentum of the chamber.

"The chamber travels at nearly the speed of light, as I said, so the local space region around the wormhole mouth is unaffected. Moreover, this process applies at every point along the wormhole, resulting in the chamber's constant velocity. It is the initial acceleration of the chamber that provides the very energy for this process to occur.

"Think of it this way: a wormhole is like a line of dominos. Set the first in motion and its energy is transmitted to the second which is then transmitted to the third which is then transmitted to the fourth—right on down the line. The chamber harnesses that energy to move through the wormhole, again, at slightly less than the speed of light."

"Hmm . . ." The reporter seemed less than convinced.

"Alternatively, consider the undulation of ocean waves. The water moves vertically, but the energy travels horizontally, giving the appearance of movement where there is none. A vessel atop the water moves along the line of energy—what is termed transverse motion—in a manner analogous to our chamber through the wormhole. You experience the effect yourself when riding waves along the shore."

The scientist smiled. "Of course, these are simple

examples. Wormhole travel is an immensely more complex process. But guided by this sophisticated device, it is now a reality."

Here the scientist paused and began adjusting the apparatus.

"I see." The reporter did not see, of course, and was in fact thoroughly confused at this point. He would have to take the scientist's points on faith.

At that moment the laboratory door opened, and a second man entered the room. Tall, thin, with wavy hair and light-blue eyes, he exuded self-confidence. He strode across the room and handed several sheets of paper to the scientist (the reporter was able to get a glimpse of the topmost sheet and saw that it was covered with scientific equations). The man looked familiar though the reporter was not sure where he might have seen him.

"My trusted assistant," the scientist said as he motioned the man to inspect one portion of the apparatus.

"Pleased to meet you," the reporter said to the assistant, who nodded but did not reply. The reporter turned back to the scientist and asked, "And where might this wormhole bridge take us?"

"Why, to the stars, of course."

The reporter raised his eyebrows. "And you believe mortals can control such a celestial phenomenon?"

With a "harrumph" the scientist walked over to an old, oak desk in a far corner of the room, sat down, and began writing feverishly, more equations, the reporter guessed, a structural analysis of the wormhole's internal dynamics, perhaps. The scientist had mentioned earlier that several minor details still needed to be worked out.

The reporter knew enough not to question the scientist further. The man's mercurial temperament was well-known. It was said people worked with him only because of his scientific brilliance, but it often came at a cost. The scientific landscape was littered with the corpses of people who had dared to question both his theories and methods. The reporter had heard of many incidents, but one in particular stuck out, one he had personally witnessed. It had been years before at the Fourth International Conference on Space Colonization which he was covering for the Times. The scientist had just delivered a paper entitled "The Physiological Effects of Extended Space Missions," when he was asked a question—the reporter no longer remembered the precise wording—which the scientist apparently felt questioned his methods. He flew off in a rage, ridiculing the poor questioner—a Ph.D. student from MIT—who turned red with embarrassment. The reporter certainly had no desire to be on the receiving end of such a tirade!

At this point the assistant took over the thread of the conversation. "From the quantum foam we extract two wormhole mouths," he said. "One here, the other at our destination. We pass an electrical charge from one to the other, effectively creating a tunnel. Using this machine"—he pointed to the device in front of them—"we can manipulate the far wormhole mouth: its speed, direction, and so forth." He smiled. "I anticipate your objection. But let me assure you, it is *not* a myth. Indeed, our universe was once a microscopic wormhole and was inflated to its current size by the great cosmic expansion of which you have so eloquently written." He was referring to the reporter's work covering cosmic inflation which had won him numerous awards.

The reporter shook his head in wonder. "Where do you intend to go?"

The scientist—who, apparently, had been listening all along—interjected, "To the planet Mythos, of course, a habitable planet recently discovered in the HD 10180-star system, some one hundred light years distant."

The reporter turned back to the assistant and asked, "What about the time it will take for such a journey? Won't that disqualify you? I'm thinking about the challenge . . ."

"The wormhole mouth travels at nearly the speed of light," the assistant said, "therefore the rate of travel through a wormhole is proportional to a Lorenz gamma factor of seven thousand four hundred fifty-five." Noticing the reporter's look of puzzlement, he explained,

"The Lorenz factor, as found in the equations of relativity, is used to calculate the degree of time dilation which is the factor by which time slows down at relativistic speeds. For the velocity of the wormhole mouth, time dilates by a factor of seven thousand four hundred fifty-five; in other words, one travels a distance of one light-year in approximately seventy minutes."

The reporter did the calculation himself. "A hundred-light-year trip in a mere five days!"

"Not only for the celestial traveler, but for those of us on Earth as well."

"How can that be?" the reporter asked.

"Though it might seem to violate common sense, it's a consequence of the laws of physics. Again, because of relativity, the dilation of time turns the wormhole into a time machine. The wormhole mouth at the far end of the wormhole is one hundred light years away, but it connects back in time to the originating wormhole mouth which is only five days away. From the point of view of an observer on Earth, the wormhole has traveled at a speed of seven thousand four hundred fifty-five times the speed of light!"

"In other words, we will be able to see the passage of events just as the celestial traveler sees them?"

"Essentially, yes. For a hundred-year trip, there will be a mere five-day delay."

The assistant pressed a small blue button on the control panel and the video screen came to life. The screen showed the inside of the chamber, now brightly lit. It contained a red leather armchair that looked as if it had been patched in one or two places. Mounted on the wall facing the chair was a clock identical to the one on the pillar. The steady ticking of the two clocks sounded almost ominous.

The assistant continued, "The clocks tick at the same rate, now and after the transportation. However, because of the Lorenz factor, one tick of the chamber's clock after its one hundred light-year journey, will equal seven thousand four hundred fifty-five ticks of our clock."

"You said the clocks always tick at the same rate."

"They do. In fact, they will still appear synchronized."

"That can only happen if the chamber's clock has moved into the future."

"Precisely."

For a moment the reporter was stunned into silence. Here he was in the twenty-first century, witnessing the dawn of a scientific revolution unlike any other! He tried to put aside thoughts of the certain Pulitzer prize that awaited him for his coverage of the event, and said, "Even so, this has never been done. And if you are wrong a man will surely die in the attempt."

The scientist spun around in his chair. "You are correct," he said. "And that is why I have decided to enter the wormhole myself."

***

The first transmissions from Mythos were thrilling. Images from another planetary world! Mythos was a rocky planet—and a wet one. The scientist had emerged in the equatorial region, in an area covered with yellow-green moss. A short distance away he came upon a series of hot-water ponds, themselves covered with a red algae-like material. The sky was milky-white—a result of the planet's thick cloud cover. There was not a breath of wind.

Up ahead he came upon a rocky prominence, perhaps fifty feet high, which he quickly ascended. A lush, green forest of trees that eerily resembled ancient Russian forest oaks stretched to the horizon. To his left lay a swampland of winding dark-water rivers and thick foliage that looked impenetrable. The area to his right was different as well. A vast grassland extended for perhaps a mile, and in the distance beyond, he glimpsed hills that were dark-red in color and peppered with large objects—boulders perhaps. He would have loved to investigate, but the towering grasses forbade entry in that direction as well.

The scientist spent the next several hours trudging over the immediate area and the adjacent forest, sampling the soil and examining rocks. His only disappointment: he saw no signs of alien fauna.

Near the forest, however, he came upon a slow-moving stream that was filled with a bubbling black liquid. Thinking this might be a sign of microbial life, he obtained a sample with a suction-lift device and ran it through his portable ion chromatograph. The results were inconclusive: the chromatograph separated the sample into a complex mixture of proteins, nucleotides, and amino acids which were similar—but not identical—to those found in microbial life forms on Titan (he had been a member of the team that made that monumental discovery nearly a decade before). The scientist knew, however, that there were a host of other explanations. Further analysis would have to await his arrival back on Earth.

He made a final circuit of the immediate area but found nothing new. He noted that the sky was still cloudy, and the air seemed thicker than before. It had also grown quite humid as if it was about to rain. Who knew what unhealthy miasma might fall from those ominous clouds? The scientist certainly didn't want to stick around to find out.

His business concluded, he packed up and entered the chamber to begin the journey home.

And that was when disaster struck.

***

"We seem to have miscalculated," the assistant said. He had been watching the video screen, carefully studying the image of the scientist's clock in the chamber. "We neglected to take into account the relativistic effects of the return voyage. Whereas travel through the wormhole is nearly instantaneous, travel back through the same wormhole is not."

At first the reporter thought the clock hands had stopped, then he realized they had not stopped but were barely moving. He raised his eyebrows. "The clocks are no longer ticking at the same rate. I thought the underlying physics was all worked out."

"We thought it was. But we failed to consider that while the process of backwash results in a near instantaneous transfer of matter through space, it is this very process that prevents the prompt return of matter through that same space. It appears to be a new property of space, or rather, a property of which we were unaware. The elasticity of space-time."

"What if you were to create a second wormhole, from Mythos to Earth?" the reporter offered.

The assistant shook his head. "Unfortunately, the construction of a second wormhole would involve the creation of a space-time causality loop. Strictly forbidden by relativity, the existence of such a loop would result in an explosion that would annihilate the universe."

"What if we first collapsed our wormhole mouth? Might not the creation of a second wormhole then be possible, one that would not violate causality and which he could use to return to Earth?"

"Unfortunately, no. If we were to collapse our end of the wormhole, the entire structure would collapse."

"And?"

"And Herr Director would be crushed. In an instant." There was an unmistakable sneer in the assistant's tone.

"We must warn him, then, so he can return to Mythos before we close our end of the wormhole."

"We can't contact him when he's in the wormhole. Nor will he return to Mythos on his own. He doesn't think anything is wrong!"

"I see." The reporter paused. "This leaves him . . ."

"Floating forever in the wormhole, unfortunately. A gruesome death."

"Then our only course of action is to close our end of the wormhole," the reporter concluded. "The structure will collapse, as you say, but it is possible he will emerge elsewhere." The reporter possessed a rudimentary knowledge of multiverse theory and knew that, while still theoretical, the existence of at least a dozen other dimensions was a distinct possibility.

"Unlikely. His body would be crushed instantaneously

by the forces generated by the wormhole's collapse." The assistant sighed. And then the edges of his mouth slowly curled in a smile that was chilling. And it was then that the reporter remembered where he had seen the scientist's assistant. At the Seventh International Conference on Space Colonization. Only he hadn't been the man's assistant at the time. He had been a researcher from Caltech. A researcher who was working in the lab of the man who had been the scientist's main competitor in the race to construct the first wormhole machine. The man who had lost.

His eyes opened wide. "Surely you aren't suggesting such a course of action?"

"It's preferable to spending a lifetime alone in the wormhole, is it not? Keep in mind that though it appears to us as if he's just entered the wormhole, he's already been inside five days."

"Surely there's something we can do, something we've overlooked. There are always alternatives."

"You can't change the laws of physics."

The reporter turned back to the video screen. "He's moving slowly, it's true," he said. "Yet he doesn't seem concerned."

"That's because to him time is passing normally. But because of the elasticity of space-time, it will take a hundred years for him to return. He will die long before then. Remember, he took only enough food to last ten days and that time has now passed. Probably he is wondering what went wrong. Soon he will grow thirsty. Within a matter of days, he will be near death. We must put him out of his misery."

Seemingly without a pause, the assistant pushed the red button.

The reporter's face went pale. "You must be mad. The man will die!"

The assistant shrugged. "He'll die anyway. And this death is preferable to what awaits him in the wormhole." Noticing the reporter's look of dismay, he added, "It *is* a pity. Perhaps he'll pop out elsewhere—we can always hope—but we'll never know. Communication with other dimensions is impossible." He smiled. "I guess you could say we're trapped in ours as well."

He flicked the power switch and the apparatus ground to a halt.

The reporter didn't know what to do. Regardless of the scientist's likely fate, this was cold-blooded murder! The assistant had no right—moral or otherwise—to take such an action. And the reporter was duty-bound to report what he had seen. Unfortunately, there were no other witnesses—it was his word against the assistant's—and he didn't like the way the man was staring at him.

It was quite a relief to the reporter, then, when the laboratory door opened, and the scientist strode into the room, a blue parrot perched on his left shoulder. He was carrying a large canvas bag marked SPECIMENS, rocks and soil samples no doubt. There was a broad smile across his face and he seemed larger than life, almost godlike. The poor assistant, however, looked as if he had just seen a most unforgiving ghost.

"As I was saying," the scientist began. "This is a most amazing apparatus. It distorts the space-time continuum, in effect altering reality . . ."

The reporter could only shake his head—and wonder.

2038: A Mars Odyssey

Frederick Hunter had the strangest dream. He was lost in New York City back on Earth. He called for help, but no one came to his aid. He hurried up and down busy streets, smelled the exhaust of cars that sped by. He went into a drugstore on one corner and asked directions to his hotel, but the man at the counter only stared at him blankly. He felt helpless.

The scene switched. His wife, Julia, was in her garden in the country, weeding. Julia had always enjoyed working in the garden. Clumps of yellow iris surrounded by rings of dainty daffodils. Rows of pretty, red and white roses in full bloom. Two forsythia bushes that blazed with brilliant yellow flowers. She loved the feel of soft, moist soil as her fingers dug out weeds. And the heavenly smells of the flowers. The sky was blue and dotted with puffy, white clouds. It was quiet, eerily so.

Julia uttered a cry. She brushed loamy soil from pieces of a blue porcelain teakettle Frederick had given her on their wedding day. "I've been looking for this teakettle for years!" she exclaimed. Just then a thin black snake poked its head from the soil in which the kettle had lain. The reptile had bright-yellow eyes, red-and-blue crosshatch markings on the body, and primitive arm-like appendages which moved about in many directions. Julia jumped away in disgust as the snake slithered away. Frantically—almost as if her life depended on it—she reassembled the pieces of the teakettle and Frederick read the following words engraved in bold, black letters: "'Till death do us part" and the date: "March 21, 2036."

He thought of this dream often in the weeks that followed, and it never failed to terrify him: what if he was to die here on Mars?

***

The day began like any other. As Frederick suited up for the trip to Chryse Planitia, he noticed that the suit's oxygen sensor was reading a fraction of a percent below normal. It didn't alarm him. It had been slightly off for days and he simply hadn't gotten around to replacing the unit.

Martian Base Alpha—mankind's first, and only, Martian outpost—was in Valles Marineres, a nearly five-kilometer-long valley that ran along the planet's equator. Chryse Planitia (the "Plains of Gold") was a smooth, circular plain at the eastern end of the valley. It was one of the planet's lowest regions and showed signs of water erosion. Apparently, water had flowed out of Valles Marineres and into the plain in the distant past. It was an excellent place to search for signs of alien life. Commanded by Captain Frederick Hunter, the outpost consisted of a dozen scientists. A second outpost, whose members were currently en route from Earth, was to be established in the south polar region.

Frederick headed out in the rover on the two-hour trip that would take him to Chryse Planitia. The sky was fiery red, the sun a bright star low in the east. The temperature was ten degrees Celsius. Balmy for this time of year.

At one point, Frederick began to feel light-headed. He

attributed it to a poor night's sleep (the recurrence of his nightmare), but as the day wore on it grew worse. He looked at his oxygen sensor; it read one percent below normal. Unless it reached six percent—highly unlikely— it was nothing to be concerned about. When he returned to the Base that evening, he would be sure to check into it. Staring up into the pale-red Martian sky he saw that it had a mosaic texture. Like the stained glass of a cathedral.

As Frederick approached the site, he slowed the vehicle to a crawl. No matter how many times he came to this place, he was always struck by its solitude. The vast, red plain littered with boulders, sinuous ridges, and dusty dunes. The emptiness that stretched to the horizon. He was two hundred million kilometers from Earth and prospecting for rocks. How thrilling it would be to become the first to discover organisms on this desolate planet!

The scientific instruments at the excavation site were designed to drill through rocks and analyze the underlying soil for signs of life. A powerful laser blasted apart rock and soil. The gas chromatograph heated the vaporized bits and separated the resulting gases into various components. The spectrometer bombarded those components with alpha particles and x-rays, then analyzed for carbon compounds. Though designed to work autonomously, the instruments needed to be periodically checked and adjusted.

Today Frederick needed to clear an area around Site 4B. He pulled a drill from the rover and went to work and as he did so his mind began to wander.

Damn! Frederick wasn't paying attention and he drilled into the side of the spectrometer. (The laser, too, was damaged, but could be repaired.) He watched in horror as the precious gases it contained seeped out. There was a replacement back at the Base, but that meant this day was wasted. He did not notice that his oxygen sensor registered two percent below normal.

As far as his current situation went, there was little he could do. Without the spectrometer, nothing could be analyzed. Further prospecting would be pointless. He began packing up and was about to climb into the rover when off in the distance he saw a flash of light. Initially, Frederick thought it was a shooting star (they were prevalent on the plain, even in the daytime), but it flashed repeatedly and at regular intervals.

With no hesitation, he made the decision to investigate.

As the rover edged towards the light, Frederick's heart was racing. When he was perhaps half a kilometer away he realized he was observing a cluster of pulsating lights. His palms began to sweat, and he found himself taking deep breaths, but he attributed it to the anticipation of the unknown.

Frederick's oxygen sensor was now six percent below normal.

He wasn't looking where he was going, and the rover struck a boulder. "Oh, God!" he cried in dismay. The rover caromed off the boulder and pitched sideways into a gully. He was thrown from the vehicle and hit his head on a second rock which, luckily, crumbled on impact. Momentarily stunned, he lay still. Then he picked himself up and brushed the red dust from his spacesuit.

He examined the vehicle—and shuddered. Several of the metal struts were bent beyond repair. Due to gravity being a mere one-third that of Earth's, he should have been able to easily right the vehicle, but one of the front wheels was wedged between two rocks and would not budge.

He radioed back to the Base and told them what had happened. He mentioned the lights that even now his eyes were fixed upon. He was told that a rescue rover could not be sent out until morning. He had no choice but to hunker down for the night—a night during which the temperature might reach minus thirty degrees Celsius.

Frederick's head was beginning to ache, and his right leg felt numb. Apparently, the fall was worse than he first thought. If he could have seen his skin, he would have observed that it had a bluish tinge.

He looked at the lights which grew steadily closer as dusk approached. They had been right about the suitability of Chryse Planitia for life, but wrong about the progression of its development. The lights were no natural phenomenon. Indicating the presence of life forms far above the microbial stage, they flashed with a meaning known only to their makers.

Frederick opened the rover's cargo bay and pulled out the damaged laser. Though no longer suitable for experimental work, it still functioned and would make a useful weapon. Then he turned to face the lights. They had increased in intensity and pulsated with a haunting blue.

Clutching the weapon, he started across the plain.

***

"Here!"

Jason McNight scrambled over the rocky caldera. After hours of searching, he had come upon the crashed rover. He radioed Peter Larissa who was searching an area about one hundred meters to the south.

Jason radioed the Base, "Rover located. Search in progress."

It was nearly noon in Chryse Planitia. The sky was pale-red, the sun a small fiery yellow globe directly overhead. They'd had no transmissions from Frederick since the night before and feared the worst.

It took several minutes for Peter to make his way over the caldera. He scanned the area as he did so and saw nothing but an endless plain studded with small, jagged boulders and twisty, narrow dunes.

Jason waved at his partner when he came into view. Peter's spacesuit was covered with red Martian dust. Larger and courser than the dust that covered the lunar surface, the dust could easily clog spacesuit filters and cover lenses. If not carefully monitored, the results could be catastrophic: the hallucinatory effects of inhaling even trace amounts of Martian dust were well-known. Was that what had happened to Frederick?

"What was Frederick doing out here, anyway?" Jason radioed. "We're way past the excavation site."

"Dunno," Peter replied. "He said he saw something— or thought he did. Maybe he got lost. Or disoriented."

Together, Jason and Peter were able to quickly right the vehicle. The hood was smashed in. The vehicle's liquid propylene, which served as temperature-regulating fluid, had pooled underneath the front axle which was bent at an awkward angle.

The men were puzzled. Frederick hadn't said the accident was this bad. He was lucky to have survived. His extra oxygen tanks would have lasted twenty-four hours and only twelve had elapsed. So, where was he?

"He must have been traveling fast," Peter said. "Look at this mess. What the devil was he doing?"

Upon opening the cargo bay, Jason let out a low whistle. He had found the extra oxygen tanks—unused. Frederick's primary tank would have run out long ago. There was a second site, which contained supplies and in which he might have found shelter, Site 2A, but it was located several kilometers away on the northern edge of the rim.

Peter shook his head in dismay. "Maybe he tried to walk to the site and got lost?"

"Where are the footprints?"

Jason was correct. Except for their own prints and the tracks of the rover, the Martian soil was undisturbed. They were about to report their findings when they saw them: bright blue lights hovering near the horizon.

"What in the world . . ." Peter gasped.

The powerful blue lights of the alien landing craft immobilized Jason and Peter before they could radio for help. A dozen long tentacles lifted them up and into the airlock. They could not move their lips, nor their limbs, and their thought processes, while still functioning, were fading and confused. Even so, they beheld the hideous visages of their captors: the thick, green torsos, the slimy tentacles, the bright multi-colored appendages, but, above all, those reptilian faces with the elongated proboscises and the compound eyes.

The men sensed an intelligence so advanced they were powerless before it. They sensed, as well, a purpose as to what was happening.

What they did not know was that their Martian odyssey was finished. Soon they would be light-years from that dusty, red planet, on a journey that would take them to a galactic zoo in a distant region of the Milky Way, there to be gaped at until the end of their days as hapless creatures from a far-flung world.

***

Frederick was nearly out of oxygen when he reached Site 2A. He stumbled through the airlock, removing his helmet as he gasped for breath. And then he collapsed.

He awoke to an unknown world. The air was dank and musty and the room he was in was illuminated by pale yellow light. His head ached. His body felt dirty, suffused with sweat. He was also quite hungry. He rubbed at his eyes and yawned. And there was another problem: *he did not know who he was.*

There was a window along one wall which looked out upon a desolate Martian landscape, the rocks a stark rusty red, the land gently rising to a hill which lay a kilometer in the distance. The landscape was forbidding, yet—to one as curious as Frederick—it was inviting as well. Mars! He remembered where he was. But not *why* he was there.

He went into a second room which appeared to be a kitchen. There he found ingredients to prepare a simple meal. As he was eating, he noticed a pantry in one corner. He opened the door and found that it was packed with food—enough to last a month or more. He rejoiced at his good fortune.

An adjacent room looked like lab space. The equipment seemed familiar, but Frederick couldn't remember what it was for. Something having to do with soil analysis, perhaps. (The thought entered his mind, but he did not know from where.) He saw several oxygen tanks along one wall and a spare spacesuit with silver-

and-gold markings.

He had seen no sign of occupants. Either this was an abandoned outpost, or the residents were outside, probably engaged in scientific work. He hitched a fresh oxygen tank to his spacesuit, put the suit back on, and emerged once again into the pale light of a cool Martian day.

The sun was nearly overhead. Though only about one-third as bright as on Earth, its light cast sharp shadows over the Martian surface. The area he found himself in was rocky with boulders ranging up to two meters in diameter. He wandered over the desiccated plain for nearly an hour but saw no one. He came upon many rock formations—some quite unusual—and was about to turn around to head back to the shelter when he saw it: two large boulders and sandwiched between them a rover, partially overturned, the front-right-side smashed in.

On the front seat Frederick found a tablet with orders from NASA. They were addressed to Captain Hunter, commander of Martian Base Alpha. Scientific investigations had revealed the existence of organic molecules in soil samples in Chryse Planitia, he read with mounting interest. Their mission was to determine if Martian microbes inhabited the area as well. And it was at that moment that memories of his past life came flooding back. *He* was Captain Frederick Hunter!

Just then Frederick heard a sonic boom. He recoiled in horror as he watched an alien spaceship swoop down out of a butterscotch sky and land in a thick cloud of Martian dust. He saw bright colors, pulsating lights, a dozen reptilian tentacles reach for two of his crewmates. He watched in stony silence as the ship rose into the sky and disappeared from view. And then he headed towards where the alien spaceship had been.

He found Peter Larissa's recorder, wedged between two rocks. He picked it up, gave it a cursory inspection, and turned around to head back.

***

It happened in an instant. Frederick didn't have a chance when six spaceships came screaming down from out of the sky. The spaceships were large, oblong, and painted bright silver. They didn't look anything at all like the other alien ship. That vessel was small, circular in shape, with vivid gold markings, a sweeping red light illuminating the cold Martian surface. These ships were cigar-shaped with a translucent dome from which a soft, yellow light pulsated. They landed in unison about one hundred and fifty meters from Frederick. He had no idea what to expect when the aliens emerged—would they also be reptilian in nature or something odder still? — and was startled to discover that they looked remarkably similar to humans. It was parallel evolution on a cosmic scale and a stunning validation of the scientific theories of Darwin.

What happened next Frederick found unfathomable: the aliens began communicating via telepathy, their thoughts simply forming in his mind. He was told to report to Spaceship 123A at eight the next morning. There was a blinding flash and the ships took off and he was alone, staring up at the structure which was Site 2A. He entered the building once again and spent a troubled night, slipping in and out of nightmarish dreams—was he to be killed? Did they want something from him?—until he could take no more and pulled himself, exhausted, out of bed. After breakfast, he examined the recorder. He pressed the playback button, but nothing happened. He shrugged, donned his spacesuit, and stepped out onto the Martian landscape.

No one was in sight. He had no idea what he was supposed to do when a series of thought transmissions—similar to those of the day before—guided him to Spaceship 123A. The ship was painted blue and gold with an image of a creature that resembled a dragon along both sides. In the middle of the spaceship was an oval hatch, bright red. As he gazed upon it, it opened. He expected one of the aliens to emerge, but no one came out. Minutes passed. Frederick realized it was up to him.

He entered hesitantly.

He felt the thumping of his heart.

His skin was cold and clammy.

He feared he would never see Mars again.

When Frederick was fully inside, the hatch closed abruptly. He jumped back startled, expecting to be confronted by aliens, but he was met only by silence.

The interior of the spaceship looked like a set of narrow white tubes that jutted out in many directions. It bore little resemblance to the structure as it had appeared from the outside, and Frederick wondered what he might have stumbled into. He wondered if he would be led to the meeting place by telepathy, but, oddly, nothing happened. He picked one of the tubes at random and began to follow it, and as he did so he felt his mind grow numb.

***

The alien's name was Abd al-Rahman al-Sufi. He claimed to be a visitor from Little Cloud, an amalgamation of over a trillion stars which was faintly visible from Mars on a moonless night. He had sparse gray hair, a long, aquiline nose, high cheekbones, fading black eyes. His brow was furrowed and there were deep creases under his eyes. He smiled when Frederick entered his cabin and motioned him to take the seat opposite. The room was spacious. Frederick saw two bronze lamps, a desk, and a black leather sofa. The walls were painted light blue. There was a drawing of a fishing village on one wall. A painting of a dozen Asian warriors slogging through a dreary mountain pass on another. A bright yellow rug adorned the floor. (He doubted these things were native to al-Sufi's world; most likely they'd gathered the information from Frederick's mind the day before.)

Frederick sat down and took a proffered glass of a red liquid which al-Sufi identified as a beverage from his home planet.

"You are Captain Hunter?"

"I am."

"You are in command of this Base?"

"Yes." Frederick paused. "I assume you are the conquerors, we the conquered?"

Al-Sufi only smiled.

"You mean you are not invaders?"

"We were too late to save your two crewmates, but I was able to shield you from the Reptilian probe."

"I don't understand."

Al-Sufi paused, then said, "We are here to save your world."

Frederick felt himself swoon as a thick fog swept over him. Flashes of bright, white light danced before his eyes. He felt the rush of a lawless wind and smelled the intoxicating aroma of wild roses. And through it all he saw al-Sufi staring at him with not a trace of emotion.

"You see," al-Sufi raised his left-index finger and made a slow circling motion. "You will be taken to another room. Later you will be free to go."

That was it? No instructions? No interrogation? Or did they mean to—

"You are to be the instrument of your world's salvation."

Frederick heard al-Sufi count to three. And that is all he remembered.

***

Frederick found himself in a room with white walls. There were drawings of fishing villages on the walls, as there had been in the room where he met al-Sufi, as well as paintings of sea towns and harbors and a picture of a lake filled with enormous reptiles. The room was lit by four brass lanterns hanging from the ceiling. He was lying on a small bed that was covered with cotton sheets. A light blue pillow supported his head. There were four other beds in the room; all empty. The door opened, and a woman entered. Her face was smooth, her complexion clear, her green eyes steady and calm. She was wearing a red skirt, and a white blouse with yellow buttons down the front. She asked how he was, but before he could respond she pulled out a butcher knife from beneath her skirt and, her green eyes gleaming, handed it to al-Sufi who had also appeared. Frederick screamed. As he lost consciousness he saw al-Sufi hovering over him, the knife raised over his head; the alien seemed to flutter in and out of existence.

When Frederick awoke, al-Sufi was the only one in the room. A misty haze suffused his mind and he was too exhausted to put up a fight. Al-Sufi touched the sides of Frederick's head where it ached and gently massaged the temples. The operation had been a success, he said. The nightmares would soon subside. He gave Frederick a few minutes to compose himself. And then al-Sufi told him what they wanted him to do.

***

"What happened to the men?" queried a reporter with the St. Louis Tribune.

"Since their bodies weren't recovered, we'll never know for sure," the government spokesman said. "As for what we believe happened . . ." Dr. George Barker was in his mid-fifties, tall and slender, with dark-brown eyes and closely-cut black hair. He was well-respected, having been involved with several investigative committees during his decade-long tenure with NASA, including the infamous Moon Base Gamma explosion that had wiped out most of mankind's first lunar settlement.

"We believe," Dr. Barker continued, "Frederick Hunter died after a spacesuit malfunction. At the excavation site he'd complained about an oxygen leak. Though less than two percent, we consider it the first indication of oxygen deprivation, particularly because he never referred to the problem again and his final transmissions indicated a heightened, almost frantic, sense of urgency. Over what, he was unable, or unwilling, to make clear.

"Jason McNight and Peter Larissa were killed by a Martian dust storm. Known as dust devils, they are the greatest threat to astronauts on the Martian surface.

They arise without warning and dissipate just as quickly. Though calm weather had been forecast throughout the day, investigation of the area in and around Site 4B indicated the possibility of foul weather earlier: increased adhesion of dust on the surface and two pairs of dust devil tracks that led to the north. Probably the men took shelter in a gully when the storm arose where they now lie covered in dust. There are hundreds of gullies all over Chryse Planitia. We'll keep looking, but chances are the men will never be found.

"The lights McNight and Larissa commented on before their final, garbled, transmissions have been attributed to a phenomenon known as a devil tower. When a devil is fast and wide enough it sucks so much dust into the atmosphere negative charges build up which result in lightning bolts dissipating in many directions. A Martian borealis, if you will. This one wasn't that large, but smaller devils have similar effects."

And as far as everyone in the room was concerned that was the end of the matter: the case was closed.

***

It was a war between two ancient civilizations. They had chased each other over space and time for a thousand years. The Reptilians hearkened from Little Cloud as well. But, unlike al-Sufi's race, which was peaceful, the Reptilians were warlike. And they intended Earth's solar system to be their next conquest. Al-Sufi's people would not permit that. Al-Sufi smiled as he concluded to an astonished Frederick, "and you will ensure that it does not happen."

***

Two weeks later war broke out. The Reptilian army crossed the northern rim of Chryse Planitia in a lightning advance, then moved to the central plateau. Martian Base Alpha fell quickly.

When contact with the outpost was lost, NASA was

concerned, but not alarmed. Any of a number of reasons could have accounted for the sudden silence. But after several more days passed with no communication, mission control grew uneasy. The second ship, the *Troubadour*, would be redirected to land in Chryse Planitia and conduct a rescue mission. That ship was one-month away. Frederick and his men would have to hold on until then.

***

With the Martian base destroyed, Frederick donned his spacesuit and journeyed to the Red Caves that bordered Chryse Planitia. There was a dry ravine, about two kilometers in length, that loped across gently sloping Martian land before rising up a hillside and ending at a clearing that provided a magnificent view of the overrun Base below. He gazed into the light-red sky as if seeking guidance from above. But none came.

When Frederick looked down he found himself staring into the penetrating eyes of al-Sufi. Frederick opened his mouth to speak, but al-Sufi brought a finger to his lips in a vain attempt to silence Frederick. Where had he come from? Frederick asked. Al-Sufi smiled. He was always watching, he said. And then al-Sufi told Frederick a story of life on Rhune, a planet that circled a star in Little Cloud.

Rhune was a swamp planet which teemed with reptiles, much like this solar system's primeval planet Venus. Except Rhune, unlike Venus, was also home to primitive man-like creatures. Hominids who were being wiped out by the slithering reptiles that seemed to be everywhere. To ensure the survival of the hominids al-Sufi's people genetically engineered them for telepathy. And with that al-Sufi touched his left temple. Immediately, Frederick felt a wincing sensation in his own temples and then a feeling of warmth flooded his mind.

We came looking for life on Mars and look what we found, he thought.

"Base Alpha has been destroyed," Frederick said. "What is the point of further resistance?"

Al-Sufi frowned. "The Reptilians next conquest will be Earth."

***

It was the moment mankind had waited centuries for: the discovery of life on other worlds. It was dubbed "The Eleventh-Hour Discovery" by the press on Earth, for, after the initial deaths were reported, and with the possible loss of the Martian base, it was understood that the colonization of the red planet had suffered a major setback, if it was not to be cancelled altogether.

On March 18, 2039, a week after Martian Base Alpha had fallen, and three weeks after Frederick and the others had vanished, one of the high-resolution cameras revealed the telltale signs of Martian life. It was in an underground cavern on the outskirts of Site 4B that organisms resembling aquatic flatworms were imaged. Bearing an uncanny resemblance to *Schmidtea mediterranea* back on Earth, the organisms had pale-white bodies and oval mouths surrounded by hundreds of hairlike projections. They secreted a sticky substance on their undersides that defied analysis.

The images were received by an astonished Earth, still reeling from the apparent loss of the first manned Martian mission.

***

When the Reptilian army was defeated, Frederick could not suppress a smile. It had been child's play! He had visualized in his mind the foreign invaders and instructed their commanders to order their battalions to fire upon their own units. It was telepathically-induced mass suicide. The soldiers were slaughtered like turkeys, blood flowing across Chryse Planitia and the central highlands. Realizing they had met their equals, the Reptilian force withdrew, never to trouble the inhabitants of Earth's solar system again.

***

In the battle's aftermath, Frederick realized that scattered over the galaxy there must have been many such as himself. It is most likely they were all part of a grand scheme, a universal life-sustaining web.

One evening Frederick went to the Base chapel, which, miraculously, had escaped the wrath of the Reptilians. There he found al-Sufi in one of the pews. The alien smiled when he saw his former pupil. Al-Sufi had aged considerably since Frederick had first seen him. He looked like an elderly man in his eighties, perhaps older; it was hard to say. His face was gaunt, his eyes tired, his body thin. There was an oak walking stick at his side. Frederick was taken aback by al-Sufi's appearance and it must have showed, for al-Sufi said, "Don't be concerned."

Frederick asked why he had aged so and al-Sufi referred to the dilation of time, a concept with which Frederick was unfamiliar. Al-Sufi said that what Frederick saw as a temporal disturbance was simply the cacophony of his own thoughts. Al-Sufi spoke then of life in higher dimensions, but Frederick could not follow his reasoning. He nodded, though, as if he understood.

Frederick asked if there were further orders, but al-Sufi did not respond. And then Frederick told al-Sufi of the vision he'd had months before, of time and space and other things, and he asked al-Sufi who he really was. Al-Sufi said a man like yourself that was all, but this didn't put Frederick at ease. He knew al-Sufi was immensely old, one thousand years or more, and he knew as well that, in the place he was from, time had no meaning. He may have been a man, or a man once, yet he was something else now and what that was Frederick would never know.

And then Frederick saw that al-Sufi was fading, like a vision that dissipates when morning comes.

He assumed al-Sufi's people left Mars then, in their silvery spaceships.

Yes, Frederick had saved Earth, but at what a price! Alone on a desolate planet, a martyr to humanity, there was one thing left for him to do.

***

Julia Hunter was in her garden, weeding. This was the place she went to when she needed to relax, when the stresses of the day threatened to overwhelm her, and after the disappearance of her husband, his presumed death, well, her life had been like a living hell. Only days before, NASA had informed her of the discovery of life on Mars. It was wonderful, of course, and Frederick would have been thrilled at the news, but it did nothing to alleviate the pain of her loss, indeed, it seemed only to have been heightened.

It was a beautiful spring day, the sky a light shade of blue shot through with streaks of pink and gold where the sun was slowly rising. The aroma of spring flowers permeated the air. Honeysuckle and bayberries. Wild roses that seemed to surround her.

Just then she heard the telephone ring. She rose and stretched her lithe body. She inhaled the intoxicating air of spring. And then she went to answer.

"Hello?"

"Julia? It's George Barker from the Johnson Space Center. We found him. Your husband. He's okay, Julia, and he says he has quite a story to tell you—to tell us all."

***

"Over here!"

A rush of feet, searchlights on full, a staggering figure illuminated. A gasp. A sign of recognition. A weak smile.

An outstretched arm caught Frederick as he fell fainting onto the fiery plain. One month after his disappearance and a kilometer from Site 2A.

An auxiliary hose was connected to Frederick's suit,

the rush of fresh oxygen slowly reviving his half-lifeless body.

And as the mist of unconsciousness cleared, Frederick recalled the vast plain of Chryse Planitia, stretching to eternity, imagined the look of horror on the faces of his friends when they were abducted, saw, as if written in gold, al-Sufi's writ ordering his protection, and, as the eyes of his rescuers settled upon him, heard the suspiration of the wind that only moments before had arisen and swept it all away.

THE MINERS OF ERIN

A man entered the bar from out of the smoky grayness of dusk. He was a handsome man, Alice thought. She liked the look of his face and hands. A strong man. She saw that his arms were long and muscular. And then there were his eyes. Enormous, blue eyes. Sad eyes. Eyes that said nothing and at the same time said everything. Eyes that looked like they might be hiding something. The man must have been in his early thirties, a bit old for the usual crowd in the bar. Most of the inhabitants of Lightning Spruce were in their mid-twenties. He seemed lost in thought. Alice wondered what he was thinking, but she was not about to ask. She had an uneasy feeling about him.

Someone called out to her from the counter. A young man with curly blond hair. Ted. One of the regulars. Ted had a crush on Alice, though she had never encouraged him. It would have angered Stu, for one thing. And it was well known what Stu had done to the last man who tried to steal his girl. It had happened six months before. Harvey Klaus was a day worker on the Thirdstone Vein in the Ceti gold mine ten miles north of Lightning Spruce. Harvey was tall and thin with light-brown hair, steely eyes, and enormous hands with long, bony fingers. He'd been mining on Erin for nearly a year and was already rich, he bragged to a pretty, young bartender named Alice Jones late one evening. To prove it he handed Alice a gold bracelet inlaid with precious gems that sparkled in the harsh light of Fisher's Bar. There was more where that came from, he told her. But the next day Harvey was found in a back alley two blocks from the bar. He had been strangled. When word of the killing got around, well, it was hands off Alice from then on. Even so, that did not prevent Ted from gazing lovingly at her whenever he got a couple of drinks in him.

Erin was the fourth planet orbiting the red-dwarf star Theia. It was a mining planet. A geologist's dream, with rich deposits of silver and gold, platinum and zinc. It had been discovered by prospectors from Earth in the year 2128. Within five years half-a-dozen towns had taken hold. Five years later the number had increased to nearly one hundred. Named after old ghost towns of the American west, there was Cerbat, Pierce, and Courtland. Hackberry, Truxton, and Valentine. Gilmore, White Knob, and Quartzburg. And Lightning Spruce. One of the first and the largest with a population of nearly twelve thousand. There was no government on Erin. It was a lawless place with towns and villages paying allegiance to governments on other planets of the Theian system, themselves originally colonized by settlers from Earth. Erin had two moons: Demeter and Arachne. They orbited once every twenty-one days at a distance of 120,000 miles, causing generally unsettled weather. Dust storms were common in the southern hemisphere and thunderstorms would go on for days in the north. But Erin was not a place where you went for a vacation. It was a place where you went to get rich. As a result, competition was fierce. It was not uncommon for fights to break out when new veins were uncovered. And with little in the way of a police force, crimes usually went unpunished. As Alice was well aware.

Alice was an attractive woman with long light-brown hair and cherry lips. Her eyes an opalescent gray. She nodded when Ted asked for an Orion Scrambler—his third—and as she was jotting down his order he asked when she was off. Would she like to see a movie that evening? *Mission to Andromeda* was playing at the Crystal Globe at 9. She smiled. She remembered the last time he had asked her out. As luck would have it, Stu had overheard. He let Ted off with a warning—he did not feel like spilling blood that night, he said—but made it clear he would not go easy on him again. He would put a knife in his back.

"I don't think so," Alice said. Even if Stu had not been in the picture she would not have been interested. Ted was nice enough, good-looking if a bit plain, a man who could always make her laugh, but he was not her type. She liked tall, handsome men, men who knew how to stand out in a room full of braggarts. Like this stranger who had entered the bar as night was falling, who strode over to the counter without acknowledging a soul, and who was motioning Alice over to him. She brought Ted his drink and then turned her attention to the stranger. The man ordered a Sonic Throbber. Those were tough to drink, Alice knew, and she admired him for trying. It showed courage and she liked that, too. She tried to read what he was thinking, read it in the lines of his face, but she came up with nothing. She looked at his hands and noticed that he was tapping the counter. And it was then she saw an ugly scar that ran across the back of his right hand from the base of his thumb to his little finger. When the man realized she was staring at his hand, he turned it over. Palm-up. He made a fist with his hand. She gazed into blue eyes, but he looked away, into the distance, the shadows of the bar. Alice had the feeling the man was here for a purpose. And not the usual one.

"Back in a second," she said.

When she brought his glass, he thanked her. He put a five-credit bill in her hand. Then he said, "Mind telling me who owns this place?"

"Jimmy Fisher," Alice replied and added, "Why do you ask?"

"Just wondered. I'd like to speak with him. If that's possible."

"He's not here."

"Know when he'll be back?"

"Nope. You never know with Jimmy. He comes and goes as he pleases."

"What do you mean?"

Alice laughed. "I mean he owns this town and he can do what he wants. That's how it works when you own something. You know? Look. Why don't you finish your drink and see what you can do in the casino room? If Jimmy comes back, I'll tell him you were looking for him. What did you say your name was?"

The man paused. "I didn't. It's Fredericks. Sam Fredericks. I'd be real grateful if you'd send him my way."

"Okay," she said. "He's a thin man with red hair. You can't mistake him. What was it you wanted to see him about, anyway?"

Sam looked at her but did not reply. Was that irritation she saw in his eyes? "I don't mean to be nosy," she said, "but Jimmy will want to know. He doesn't speak to just anyone. In fact, he's quite particular about whom he speaks to these days."

Sam looked puzzled. "Why is that?"

"Ever since the summons came down, I guess."

"What summons?"

"The brawl two months ago. In this very room. A man was killed."

"I see."

"Jimmy wasn't real happy about that as I'm sure you can imagine. Not that he did anything wrong, mind you. It wasn't his fault things got out of control. Not Jimmy. They don't come any straighter than him. He's got a temper, I'll grant you that. But who doesn't around here? You need a temper in this town just to survive. And the police needed someone to blame."

Just then Alice heard the rumble of thunder in the distance. She went over to the front window and looked out and she saw thunderclouds curtaining the sky. The wind was picking up and she saw flashes of lightning.

"I'm not going out there," she said.

"When are you off?"

"Probably about the time the storm hits. Guess I'll hang around until it's over."

"You live far from here?"

"About a mile out of town. It's okay. I'll wait."

"It might be awhile."

Alice shook her head. "Summer storms are always brief. Hey—you're not from around here are you?"

"No, I'm not."

"Where are you from then?"

Sam did not reply. He was looking at Ted who

was looking at Alice, an expression of annoyance on his face.

"Guess I'd better go," Sam said.

He finished his drink and made his way into the casino room. With its dark paneled interior and smoky atmosphere, the place seemed to beckon. As his eyes adjusted to the dim light of the room, he saw the gaming tables with people crowded around them and the cyber-slot machines and a bar. A stage where men and women were dancing. Techno-music was blaring. The synthesized sounds of the band throbbed in his skull. The pulse of multi-colored-laser light gave the room an ethereal glow. Light beams bounced off the walls to the beat of the music and reflected off people and objects alike. There was a movie screen along one wall showing a picture of an alien invasion from another galaxy, but no one was watching.

A woman brushed by Sam and he smelled her perfume. *Like a Thorian flower garden,* he thought. Her black hair fell past her shoulders. Her skin looked smooth and soft. Sam looked around and he saw more women and he saw men ogling them and he saw men gambling. He heard snippets of conversation, all of it inane. A woman came up to him and asked if he would like to dance. He smiled. "Maybe later," he said. She laughed. "Okay." And then she disappeared. She was pretty enough, that was for sure, but Sam was not interested. Not now. Now, there was something else he needed to do. There was something else he needed to do while he waited for Jimmy.

Within two hours Sam had hit the jackpot at a dozen cyber-slot machines and had won every game of Spitbacon, Rubberlance, and Metzki he had played. He had won so much money, in fact, that he had become the center of attention. Everyone was watching him. Everyone was watching and wondering what he would do next. You did not clean this place out and get away with it.

Sam was about to play one more game—all his winnings against the casino itself, he said—when from out of a back room strode a brawny man in a white linen suit, with sneering lips and caterpillar brows, his hair slicked back, his black eyes dancing. He must have been a man who commanded respect for a hush descended over the room. Everyone stopped what they were doing and watched in anticipation as the man went up to Sam and tapped him on the shoulder.

"I'm sorry, sir," the man said, "but I'm going to have to ask you to leave."

Sam didn't say anything. He looked at the man as if he was crazy. The man continued, "If you please, sir."

Sam said, "Who are you?"

The man pulled himself up to his full height. Even so, he was a good two inches shorter than Sam. "Name's Frank Williams." He pronounced the words crisply, as if they were supposed to mean something to Sam, but of course Sam had no idea who Frank Williams was. He said, "Pleased to meet you, Frank. I understand a man by the name of Jimmy Fisher owns this place. I'm waiting to see him. And I'm going to stay here until I do."

Beads of sweat appeared on Frank's brow. *If Jimmy was here he would not stand for this*, he thought. *Not for a moment.* He put his arms akimbo and said, "Sir, it's time for you to go."

"I'm not through," Sam said sharply.

"Oh, but you are," Frank replied angrily. "And," he continued, stabbing the air with his right index finger, "I'd like you to return the money you've won before you leave. No questions will be asked."

Sam raised his eyelids. "You think I'm cheating?"

"I'd never accuse you of something so dishonorable."

"I've won everything honestly," Sam said. He paused, then added, "However, if I hadn't removed those magnets under this wheel—" He pointed at the Metzki wheel.

"You're not from around here are you?"

Sam smiled. "People seem to think I'm not."

Frank scoffed. "You think you're smart, don't you?" He ran a hand through his thick, black hair and smacked his lips. "No, you're not from Erin. And we don't like otherworlders."

"I'll leave when my business is concluded," Sam said. "Erin is a mining planet. It's nothing but otherworlders. And besides, I'm just passing through."

"Get out!" Frank raised his right arm threateningly. "Or must I have you thrown out?"

Sam smiled. "As you wish. But we'll let Jimmy decide about my winnings when he returns."

Frank glowered but said nothing more. In all his years at the bar, he had not come across anyone like this man. Most people slunk away without a word when he confronted them. They knew what they were up against. And they valued their lives. But to tell the truth, Frank was scared this time. He would let Jimmy handle Sam when he got back. Jimmy would know what to do. He always did.

Sam went back out to the barroom. He went over to the counter and sat down and ordered another drink.

Alice was off now, but she could not leave Sam. She went into a back room and changed her clothes and then she came out to the counter—to the other side of the counter—and sat down next to him. Sam looked at her. She was wearing a dark-red blouse with a picture of a dragon on it, and a short, black skirt with a narrow silver belt. A bracelet around her left wrist. Her legs were long and slender, and her hair looked almost green in the pale light of the room.

Alice said, "Mind if I join you?"

He nodded. She sat down. The new woman on duty asked if she could get them anything. Sam ordered a Black Jullian. Alice, a Pink Froth. The woman wrote down their order and left. Sam said, "What's your name?"

"Alice."

"Alice what? I like to know a woman's full name when I'm speaking to her."

"Alice Jones."

"Hello, Alice. Pleased to meet you."

"You're really good, Sam. And Frank is such an idiot."

"You watched us?"

She nodded. "Everyone did. Frank is Jimmy's cousin, you know. He works for Jimmy. He's supposed to keep accounts, but most people think he doesn't do anything. Most people think Jimmy is indebted to him for some reason. Stu—my boyfriend—told me Frank helped Jimmy out of a jam once, but he wouldn't say what happened. I got the impression it was something illegal, just from the tone of Stu's voice. I think Stu might have been involved in the whole mess, but like I said, Stu hasn't told me. I know Stu doesn't like Frank and he says Frank doesn't like him, either. If you ask me, Frank is just a prick."

Sam was silent. Alice said, "Has your girlfriend run out on you?"

He shook his head. "I don't have a girlfriend."

She frowned. "I think I understand you. You want someone, but she doesn't want you. That's sad."

Their drinks arrived, and they sipped at them.

Then Sam said, "How old are you, Alice?"

"Twenty-four. And you?"

"Thirty-two."

"That's a nice age."

"You look like you're eighteen."

"I'll take that as a compliment."

A pause. Then Sam said, "How old are you, really?"

"Twenty-four. Honest."

"Right." He eyed her closely. "Your family lives here?"

"I was born on Tau. My parents divorced when I was sixteen and after a few months I fell for Stu. He told me Erin would make us rich."

"What do you see in Stu, anyway?" Sam asked. There was a puzzled expression upon his face.

"I don't know," she said after a moment's hesitation. "I like his looks, I guess."

"That's what you care about?"

"I'm a simple girl. Easy to please."

Sam said, "No, you're not. You're not easy to please."

Alice fidgeted nervously. She stared at the wall behind the counter. She seemed to be reading the menu—or else she was lost in thought. When Sam spoke again, he pronounced the words slowly, crisply, "You know who Stu is, don't you?"

"What do you mean?" Her hands were sweating, the color draining from her cheeks. Sam spit out the words, "Stu killed a man in this bar two months ago. A man named Edward Quinn. A man who happened to be my friend."

"Oh." She spoke in a watery whisper.

"And Jimmy's protecting Stu."

"Why would he do that?"

"Because Stu is Jimmy's friend."

Alice's heart was hammering. She looked out the

window into the darkness. She closed her eyes. When was Jimmy coming back?

"Quinn was a miner from the Orion star system," Sam continued. "He'd prospected the Gazensky asteroid belt as well as the planets Thor-6 and Alpha-Psi, wherever he could find work. He had a family to support and when you have a family to support you do what you have to do. He was a good man, a kind and just man. We met on Alpha-Psi, a rough planet on the edge of the Orion system. He saved my life once. We were heading home from work and were jumped by two thugs wielding knifes. We took our blows"—he pointed at his scar—"but our attackers got the worst of it. One of the men was killed, the other was wounded but managed to get away. I found out later the men were brothers. Stuart and Carlos Kennedy. Quinn left shortly thereafter—he was drawn to this planet by the prospect of easy money—and I vowed that if I ever saw him again I'd be sure to repay him. When I learned of his death at the hands of Stu, I knew I had to come here. Death doesn't absolve us of our debts, no matter where we may be."

"I know Stu is no angel," Alice said. "I'm not dumb, Sam. I know what goes on around this town. But he loves me. Okay? And I'll take Stu, warts and all. He's not like the other men in this place. Men who want you for the night. And want you to leave in the morning. You know what I mean?

"And, like I said, I know about the brawl. I wasn't there, but people told me what happened. A drunk got in a fight; one thing led to another. People said so many fists were flying it wasn't clear what happened. It was probably an accident. Those things happen. Out here on the edge of nowhere they happen all the time."

Alice finished her drink and Sam ordered her

another and while she was waiting he looked around the room. He listened to the wind howling outside. He heard the branches of a tree rubbing against the windows. Alice looked at Sam as if she expected him to say something, but he said nothing. The soulful sounds of a techno song floated through the air from out of the casino room and filled the silence between them.

Alice sighed. "You'd think—"

"Hey, man." Someone grabbed Sam by the shoulder and spun him around. "What do you think you're doing?"

"We were just talking," Sam said.

"Stu!" Alice cried, recognizing her boyfriend.

"Stay out of this, baby."

"But he's right. That's all we were doing."

"He wants your ass. Look at the bastard."

"No, Stu, please."

"Shut up."

Sam said, "Alice is right: we were just talking, okay?"

"Don't give me that crap," Stu said. "Just get the hell out of here."

Sam rose. "As you wish." He paused, then added, "And if Alice wants to, she's coming with me."

Stu pulled a knife.

Alice screamed.

Someone cried out, "Oh, Christ. Everybody look out!"

Sam looked at Stu and he looked at the knife. And then he frowned. But he did not look scared. Stu did not know what was going on, but he did not like it. He was used to people turning tail when he confronted them. Nobody faced him down and got away with it. Nobody. But as he looked into Sam's steel-blue eyes he saw the look of a man who was not about to back down. And for a moment, he felt the coldness of fear. But only for a moment. He ran his hands through his thick brown hair. He spat on the floor. He looked at Sam icily. And then he said, "Chicken." Every muscle in Sam's body was taut. The veins on his neck stood out. He ran his tongue over thin, dry lips. A lawless wind was slamming in from the south and it rattled the windows, shook the walls. A flash of lightning lit up the place as if it was daytime.

Sam looked towards the window and then he looked at Stu. His foot tapped the floorboards steadily. "Hear that?" Sam said. "Hear it?"

Stu said, "Get out." He ran the blade of the knife slowly across his throat.

Alice had never seen Stu like this, not even when he had confronted that man from up north, the man Stu thought was trying to undercut him. Then he was merely angry, but now he seemed like a man consumed by rage. The blade of Stu's knife gleamed in the light cast from the lightning bolts that lit up the room and Alice saw blood on it. Blood that was not there. Sam said, "Put that away."

"Get your ass out of here." It was Frank, emerging from the casino room. He leaned against the doorway, an expression of contempt upon his face. Filled with renewed bravado, his thick hands seemed eager to kill. Sam looked at Stu and he looked at Frank, but he did not move.

"I think you'd better do as the man asked." A voice from the counter. Sam turned and he saw Ted smirking. "You care for your life, you'd better get out of here right now." His words were slurred and his eyes bloodshot. "And as for Alice . . ." His words trailed off.

Sam looked at Alice and said, "Let's go." Alice did not reply. She was trembling. Sam guessed that she did not know what to do, but when he looked at her more closely he saw that he was mistaken. She knew what to do. Maybe for the first time in her life she knew what to do. But she was scared. "Let's go," Sam repeated, "after I've done what I came here to do."

"I've had enough," Stu said, and he spat on the floor. He took a step towards Sam, his knife at the ready.

Alice cried out, "No!"

Just then the lights went out and the music stopped. People started screaming. Someone threw a punch and moments later a fight had broken out. It happened so fast that for a moment Alice did not realize what was happening. She heard the cries of men and of women, saw ghostlike silhouettes, eyes glowing in the darkness. A bottle grazed her chest and she fell to the floor.

It was thirty minutes before the power came back on and order was restored. Chairs had been overturned, broken glass was everywhere. The smell of blood hung in the air. Men lay sprawled on the floor, many of them with cuts and bruises. Alice lay among them. Her blouse was ripped and there were marks on her face and hands.

Sam had vanished. And in the middle of the room, face down in a pool of blood, was the body of Stu. A knife was embedded in his back.

Sam disappeared from Lightning Spruce and was never heard from again. The investigation into Stu's death was inconclusive. Most people thought Sam had killed him, of course, but others were not so sure. Some thought it was Ted or even Frank. They had motives as well and it did not help that they maintained a stony silence whenever the subject was brought up.

The funeral was held two days later and was well-attended. Whatever people thought of Stu, he had quite a reputation and needed to be put to rest with respect, they said. Alice watched emotionless. She did not think anyone deserved to die, at least not in the shameless way Stu had been dispatched, but she knew what people meant when they said he deserved it.

Blood was to be spilled that fateful evening—a natural consequence of events set in motion when Sam entered the bar—the only question was whose. And that depended on Alice. Stu laughed when he saw her lying on the floor, did not notice the weapon clutched in her left hand, saw only the anger in her eyes. He dismissed her with a smirk, then turned to face Sam. A final confrontation.

What happened next was like a dream to her now. A woman slowly rising. An arm outstretched. A hand hovering in midair poised to strike the fatal blow. What would Stu have felt if he'd pivoted to face his attacker? Surprise—or humiliation? He certainly would not have expected a woman to wield the knife.

When the funeral was over, she headed home. It was a warm, windless evening. As she walked, she looked up at the night sky, at the unfamiliar stars, so bright and faraway, the twin moons that circled Erin in a passionate embrace. High overhead, she saw the faint outlines of the Andromeda galaxy. Little Cloud—as it was known—was two and a half million light years away, yet, tonight it seemed much closer. She walked on awhile longer, by the river that wound along the outskirts of town, wondering what would become of Sam and realizing that she already missed him.

BARNEGAT INN

I am a middle-aged man of fifty-six, happily married for thirty-odd years, with two fine children who have made their parents proud. The following incident occurred on my wedding day. It has haunted me ever since and, though I vowed never to set it down, the passage of time has made it seem less ominous, so I do so now.

The reader will note that the inn was located not in Barnegat, but several miles outside the town. I returned to the area once many years later. My wife was recovering from a bout with the flu and I'd taken her to her sister's house in upstate New Jersey to convalesce. I was making my way back down the coast to our home in central Virginia. It was on a whim that I detoured to Barnegat to see if I could resolve certain points that had always puzzled me, but I found no trace of the shoddy old mansion. I was certain of its location—the intersection of Highway 9 and Waverly Place—but found the land there wild and desolate without trace of structure or foundation. The inn simply was not there.

Somehow it seemed quite fitting.

***

We were married in Norfolk, Virginia, at All Saints Episcopal Church about five miles from Broad Bay. I was twenty-five years old, my dear Marianne twenty-three. It was a beautiful October morning, the sky deep blue with puffy white clouds that slowly drifted across the eastern sky. The wedding had been a small affair, immediate family and a few close friends. The priest was named Father Krone. He was a thin man, well along in years, with a long beard that grew high on his cheeks, thinning white hair, a prominent forehead, and light-blue eyes that twinkled. He was soft-spoken, yet his words held us rapt.

Though Marianne and I had met Father Krone several times, we did not know him well. He was picked to conduct the ceremony by Marianne's parents, who lived in Norfolk, attended the father's church, and whose praise of the priest was effusive.

After we said our "I do's" we exited the church through a hail of rice. My beloved was radiant in a lavender dress embroidered with pale-white flowers. I wore a light-brown suit with a bright tie.

The reception was highlighted by a six-layer chocolate cake with white frosting decorated by Marianne's mother. After changing into our regular clothes, we made our way to the church parking lot. Someone had sprayed JUST MARRIED in white letters on the rear window of our aging blue Buick and half-a-dozen tin cans dangled from the tailpipes.

I said, "Let's get going."

We swung onto Shore Drive and headed west towards the Chesapeake Bay Bridge-Tunnel. Once across we continued north on Route 13 stopping at the Virginia-Maryland border for lunch. From there we continued on Route 113 traversing the pretty Maryland countryside. A stop at Assateague State Park took up most of the afternoon. We marveled at the wild ponies that freely roamed the beach and sand dunes.

Leaving Delaware, we had dinner at a seafood restaurant in Smithville, New Jersey. We poked around Smithville before heading north on Route 1, with stops at Fenwick Lighthouse and Cape Henlopen State Park. The ferry at Cape Henlopen took us across Delaware Bay to North Cape May. We followed Route 9 along the flatlands and marshes of eastern New Jersey, and it was nearly seven in the evening when we pulled into the town of Barnegat, looking for a place to spend the night.

Barnegat was a charming seaside town on Little Egg Harbor. Across the water rose Barnegat Lighthouse. Marianne made me promise we would visit in the morning.

The first inns we came upon were full and Marianne grew worried. "We should have made reservations, John," she lamented.

"Worst comes to worst," I said, "we keep going. We'll make it to the city by midnight." I drew her to me and kissed her cheek.

Marianne had always wanted to visit New York City and I'd promised her several days in the Big Apple as part of our honeymoon. Then, on to our final destination, Bangor, Maine, where we'd rented a cottage on the outskirts of the city.

But the immediate problem was finding lodging for the night. We left Barnegat heading north on Route 9. Three miles out we saw it: a three-story red brick inn surrounded by an old wrought-iron fence. A rickety wooden sign read: The Inn at Barnegat. The grounds were unkempt. A winding gravel path bordered by pale yellow and white flowers led through the gate and up to the inn which looked abandoned.

"It can't hurt to take a look, don't you think?" I said and without waiting for a reply drove onto the inn grounds.

Ivy clung to the bricks and gray-green moss was creeping across a shingled roof. There were a dozen casement windows on the west and south sides. Smoke rose from a chimney on the east.

"At least someone's home," Marianne said.

The front door was opened by an elderly man wearing shoddy clothes. He was thin, with a grey beard, light-blue eyes, and an elf-like face. Behind him stood a woman of similar years, presumably his wife. Her long grey hair fell to her waist; it looked soft as silk. The man smiled warmly.

"May I help you?"

***

Though we were dog-tired and wished only to turn in for the night, out hosts insisted we join them in the living room by a roaring fire. We were surprised to find ourselves the only guests. Marianne told our hosts—who identified themselves as Mr. and Mrs. Smith—of our failure to find lodging in the town of Barnegat. They did not seem surprised.

"It's such a romantic place," Mrs. Smith said. "Near the sea and popular with the young folk."

When I asked why there were no other guests our hosts shrugged but said nothing.

Looking around the room, I noticed the furniture was a strange mixture of styles that spanned the ages. (My father was an antiques collector and I'd picked up a fair amount of knowledge of the field over the years.) I saw an eighteenth-century dining table made of varnished mahogany; William and Mary style chairs with tall, narrow backs and Spanish feet; a colorful braided rug from India; an oak roll-top desk of Oriental design, nestled against one of the walls.

Another of my father's interests was time pieces; he had a collection of several dozen ranging from modern to antique. Imagine my surprise when, resting on the desk, I saw an architectural wonder: a Japanese mulberry pillar clock, dating from the mid-nineteenth century. Pillar clocks (my father owned one) were fascinating devices. They indicated time on a pendulum weight instead of a clock face. As time passed, the weight dropped past a series of markings indicating the hours.

What was most interesting was the division of temporal markers: Japanese timekeeping divided the day and night into six equal periods; these 'hours' varied in time according to the season. Aside from my father's clock, I'd never seen another.

Ah, but it was the architecture of the room that alarmed me. The doors—there were three—hung at odd angles, the glass in the windows was of a type I'd never seen, dark and shimmering and oddly reflective. And the walls. The walls leaned crazily forwards, backwards, and sideways. An architectural horror. It was a wonder the room had not collapsed!

Mr. Smith spoke. "Tell us about yourselves," he said, and without waiting for a reply added, "Let me guess. You have recently married!"

At first, I was taken aback, then I realized he must have seen the lettering on our car that announced the event.

Marianne smiled. "Only this morning."

Mrs. Smith turned to her husband. "Such a lovely couple aren't they dear?"

"Quite."

"Do you attend the university?"

"The University of Virginia," I replied. "I'm a graduate student in astronomy. Marianne is pursuing a master's degree in early childhood education."

At this Mr. Smith shot up as if he'd been struck by a bolt of lightning.

"Astronomy!" he cried. "Why, then, you and I have something in common!"

"Are you a lover of the stars?"

"You could say so, yes. And you?"

"I'm working on my dissertation—on the physics of black holes."

"Isn't that a coincidence!" Mr. Smith was becoming more animated by the minute.

I was taken aback. Surely this elderly gentleman was not embarking upon a similar study. "I'm not sure I understand—"

"Let's just say it's a hobby of mine. The stars. And

since you've come to our inn, I must take advantage of the opportunity your visit presents."

I found his odd diction disturbing and I began tapping my fingers on the arm of my chair. A nervous tic of mine.

He smiled. Then he threw a dart. "Do you believe in life on other worlds?"

"No one knows for certain," I said after a moment's hesitation. "It seems likely, but—"

"Well I *do* know," Mr. Smith asserted. "And I can state categorically that life exists elsewhere in the universe."

"Really? I don't see how you can make such an assertion."

"On probabilistic grounds alone, it is a near-certainty. And to deny it now after—"

"My husband is opinionated," Mrs. Smith interrupted, "as you can tell. But what he means is—"

"I mean exactly what I have said!"

"If you mean biological life," I said, "I couldn't agree with you more. But to make the leap from cellular organisms to conscious entities—well, I think that is a leap of faith. I agree with you, though, in one respect. I believe the universe is far more exotic than anyone imagines."

"And so, it is," Mrs. Smith intoned.

"Oh—" Marianne stifled a cry.

"I mean that it would *appear* to be so," Mrs. Smith corrected.

"Even when she speaks plainly she sounds odd," Marianne whispered.

"Frank," Mrs. Smith said. "We've been such poor hosts. Surely our guests are thirsty after their long day—and we've offered them nothing. Shouldn't you be in the kitchen getting drinks?"

"How right you are!" He rose from his chair and shuffled out the room.

"Let me ask Mrs. Smith a question," my wife said. "Tell us about your lives. Did you marry when you were young?"

"We were about your age I'd say," Mrs. Smith replied.
"Advice for the newlyweds?"

She smiled. "Our twenties were our best years," she began, "carefree and full of wonder. The thirties were something else. Raising children took all of our time. By the time we reached the end of that decade we were plum worn out! The forties were a time of renewal, the challenges of childrearing easier to handle and—thankfully—occurring less often. The fifties were wonderful, the sixties even better, the seventies a decade of adventure, the eighties a glorious epoch, the nineties—"

"My, my," Marianne interrupted if only to stop Mrs. Smith who seemed likely to go on forever. And then she whispered into my ear, "John, they don't look a day over sixty."

Mr. Smith returned with a teapot from which steam was slowly rising. He poured a clear, sweet-smelling liquid with a hint of lemon. It was also soporific, apparently, for Marianne and I soon began yawning.

"Let us take up a different topic," continued Mr. Smith who seemed to positively relish the conversation. "Time travel."

"Frank," Mrs. Smith said. "Our guests didn't come here to listen to your silly theories, you know."

"Quite right." He turned to face us. "Forgive me. It's just that I seldom have the opportunity to engage in scientific conversation. Living alone as we do our minds tend to wander. Is it but a small leap of faith to imagine that our bodies do as well?" His blue eyes sparkled.

I began to wonder if, in addition to being friendly, our hosts were also demented.

"Let us consider the following," he continued with hardly a pause. "What are the implications of instantaneous temporal transfer?"

On hearing those words, I was positively ruffled. The principle of causality strictly forbids such nonsense.

"It's well-known that time travel is theoretically impossible," I said. "The speed of light is an absolute."

Mr. Smith frowned. "But a Mr. H. G. Wells has

constructed such a machine," he said, "and used it to travel to your distant past and future."

I looked at him strangely. "That was only a story."

"Oh, yes." My host looked chagrined.

"What he means, if I may interrupt," Mrs. Smith said, "is that time travel has been much discussed in your world."

"Yes, yes," Mr. Smith said. "That is what I meant."

Except, of course, that was *not* what he meant. And as I studied him closely, I noted his eager, almost aggressive eyes, his tight facial muscles, his hands clenched so firmly that the knuckles were white.

He rose from his chair, crossed the room, and stoked the fire which had died down. Moments later it was blazing brightly. He made a circle with the middle finger and thumb of his left hand and bisected the circle with the index finger. He did the same with his right hand. Then he held his hands together so that the tips of the index fingers touched. Finally, he held his hands before the light of the fire and I saw to my amazement the image of an otherworldly creature with two monstrous eyes, an enormous forelimb, and four spindly legs, cast upon the opposite wall. He was goading me, to put it plainly, and I could not let the matter stand.

"There's something strange about this place," I said, ignoring a look of caution from Marianne. "It's in the middle of nowhere. The furniture has been assembled by someone with no understanding of aesthetics. And I don't for a minute believe you're a budding astronomer."

"Dear me," he replied. "I thought. . ."

Marianne's cautionary look had turned into a frown and I said nothing further.

My wife said, "It's been a long day. We really must be heading off to bed."

"But our talk has only just begun," protested Mr. Smith who seemed not to realize that any time had passed.

"Yes, we must go," I said, and in an attempt to atone for my earlier outburst for which—to tell the truth—I was embarrassed, I added, "but thank you for your hospitality. It's been a marvelous evening."

And with that we rose. Mrs. Smith took us upstairs to a room on the third floor. The bridal suite, she said with a smile. When we passed the second-floor landing I noticed a bronze statue of Aphrodite, perhaps four feet tall, next to a casement window. It was an interesting sculpture to be sure, but, like everything else in the inn, seemed out of place.

The furniture in the bridal room was from a variety of time periods. There was a modern king-sized bed with a plain mahogany headboard, an antique nightstand that looked to date from the eighteenth-century, and several pieces I couldn't place, including a futuristic-looking sofa upholstered with a soft, white material that I'd never encountered. The bed was turned down and looked inviting. When I turned to thank our hostess, she was gone.

***

It was two in the morning—according to the clock on the nightstand—when I was awoken by a loud sound. I got up and went into the hall.

I heard voices, soft and gentle, emanating from below. I tip-toed down the stairs to the second-story landing and crouched behind the statue. Here I could not easily be seen, but I could view the living room. Around a table were gathered Mr. and Mrs. Smith and another elderly couple whom they addressed as Mr. and Mrs. Jones. I tried to listen to the conversation, but their voices were so low I heard only snippets.

". . . do us good to return home, Frank," Mrs. Smith was saying.

"The visit was worthwhile," Mr. Smith said. His next words were inaudible.

"And how was your journey?" Mrs. Smith asked, looking at Mr. Jones.

Mr. Jones was a robust man, with thinning grey hair, a wide nose, and jet-black eyes. He told a fragmentary—and fantastic—story of a trip that evening "through the heavy fog." His wife nodded as he spoke but said nothing. There was something odd about Mrs. Jones, but I couldn't put my finger on it. Perhaps her wistful, dreamy, expression, her long arms, and even longer legs, which seemed not to go with the rest of her body. Or was it the aura of otherworldliness that hung over her? Indeed, as Mr. Jones went on with his tale she seemed to slowly fade away, but later her body regained its substance and I wasn't so sure. "That fog," Mr. Jones was saying, "that fog."

And now it was I who was baffled. The night had been clear; the sky full of stars. I opened the window and poked my head out. I was comforted to see the Big Dipper and Jupiter which hung low in the western sky. Indeed, the sky was darker than it had been earlier in the evening. Then a half-moon had been shining brightly. Now it had set, and the full glory of the heavens was revealed. And it was then I realized that I saw no earthly lights. The lights from Barnegat to the south and Waretown to the north. Even the lighthouse beam seemed to have gone missing.

I was jolted back to the scene below by a sudden flash of light. Someone had lit a lantern which burned with a soft blue flame that seemed to grow stronger as the four wayward travelers stared fixedly upon it. Mr. Smith said some words in a language I couldn't understand. Then they rose and held hands, forming a circle around the lantern.

The room took on a bluish hue, then began to spin, faster and faster until I could no longer make out the forms of my hosts and their friends. And as I watched, I saw a kaleidoscope of color and forms that shifted as the seconds passed, a sphere of mind-boggling extent, a void that arose out of everything and yet itself was nothing. And all the while everything was interspersed with the outlines of a room I knew must still be there. And in that room, in which I had passed a tedious hour, I saw only the clock—the Japanese pillar clock—its hands spinning wildly forward and backwards, as if, in the space below, time had lost all meaning. There was a blinding flash of light. Then, nothing but whiteness.

When my eyesight returned I was amazed to find the room as it had been at the beginning—except that no one was there. For the briefest of seconds, I thought of investigating, but I was too shaken at this point. And so, I climbed the stairs to our room on the third floor and slipped into bed. Marianne, roused from peaceful dreams, sighed and encircled me with her arms. I felt the comforting warmth of love and soon was fast asleep.

***

When Marianne and I awoke the next morning, we found the inn enveloped in fog. We dressed, packed our bags, and went downstairs.

All was silent.

My wife called to our hosts, but no one answered.

"That's strange," she said.

"Maybe they're outside?"

"Where on earth would they go? In this fog, I mean."

I didn't say a word about the events of the previous night. I'd done my best to convince myself it had been a dream, a vision caused by the drink I'd imbibed, though, to be honest, I wasn't sure.

Marianne opened the front door and called out to the Smiths, but a blast of wind pushed her back inside.

"What do you think our hosts were trying to tell us last night?" she said.

"I don't really know," I said. "Time is precious or something like that."

She smiled and took my hand. We waited perhaps an hour, perhaps longer, for the wind to die down, and when it had abated, we picked up our bags, opened the front door, and disappeared into the morning mist. We put our things in the Buick and started off.

When the car reached the bottom of the driveway, Marianne uttered a cry. "My sandals," she said. "I left them in our room."

I stopped the car, intending to drive back to the inn, but evidently, we'd left too soon for the fog had increased in intensity and I found that the driveway was disappearing before my eyes. The lodge, visible only in outline, seemed to fade in and out of existence with the wind that had arisen once again.

"Are you certain—" I began, when Marianne interrupted, "No, here they are." She pulled a pair of red dress sandals from under the front passenger seat.

I smiled. I put the car into drive and we inched forward, into a dense fog that would not lift until we reached the town of Lakewood thirty miles to the north, a trip which should have taken a mere forty-five minutes, but which, due to the dismal conditions, took far longer. All along the route I heard the howling of an unruly wind that swirled around us, and I saw—or thought I saw—the images of our hosts smiling beneficently upon us.

When we reached Lakewood, the fog lifted for good. The remainder of our journey was without incident. I never did tell Marianne about the visitors our hosts had entertained that night, nor the strange sensations that followed me the next morning. I did, however, resolve to hold the hand of my beloved that day and for all the days that followed, however short or long.

THE WORMS OF TITAN

Titan is a dark place, its surface one-tenth as bright as Earth. The daytime temperature is about ninety-eight kelvins. Titan's atmosphere is composed primarily of nitrogen (ninety-seven percent) and methane (two percent), with the remainder consisting of trace amounts of noxious elements such as hydrogen cyanide. A forbidding world, certainly, but one teeming with organic compounds, many deep within lakes that cover much of the surface, and which make human exploration difficult. It was a welcome surprise, then, when early in 2186 the first rovers discovered those same compounds near the superstratum of Titan's rocky regions.

The Titan Life Project, as it was known on Earth, was the brainchild of Dr. Raul Ravencroft. Raul was a brilliant and ambitious man in his early fifties, with a Ph.D. in astrogeology from Caltech. He had short, curly black hair, sparkly light-brown eyes, and a slightly hooked nose. A tall, imposing man with a booming baritone voice, he walked with a limp, the result of a motorcycle accident when he was nineteen.

A decade of planning ensued, and after an uneventful year-long journey, a team of three dozen scientists and engineers landed on that mysterious world. Most of Titan was covered with methane lakes, but within thirty degrees of the equator, where Base Alpha was located, it was relatively dry. The usual robot swarm had prepared the base. Three facilities were constructed: living quarters, science labs, and engineering—nearly a square kilometer of habitable space enclosed in a pressurized bubble. It utilized technology similar to that employed in the construction of bases on Mars and Europa.

Six months later, the crew of Hovercraft TRI-2 was traveling from Base Alpha to the Adiri Plateau, a bright feature just west of a larger dark region known as Shangri-La. It was a forty-five-minute trip. There had been a report the previous afternoon of an important discovery from drilling station Gamma-24. Or rather, of *a discovery*; its importance would be for the crew to determine.

The terrain was flat and littered with boulders and pebbles. There were hills in the distance, but because of the constant methane fog they were rarely visible. There were few craters, no mountains to speak of.

Ken Swift was at the controls. Almost two meters tall, thin as a reed, with a mop of red hair, Ken hailed from the Europa colony. There he had managed a fleet of hovercraft and had serviced the robots that helped run the colony. He was twenty-eight years old, unmarried.

Martha Bell was gazing out a porthole at the harsh landscape as they rumbled by. It never ceased to amaze her: hydrocarbon dunes formed by gentle easterly winds, and rocks composed of frozen methane and water ice. Martha was in her mid-thirties, a frosty woman, with shoulder-length dark-brown hair and hazel eyes. She'd earned a Ph.D. in astronomy from Stanford a decade before and later taught in the physics department at UC Berkeley. Bell was an expert—the expert—on the moons of the outer solar system.

Jacob Fry was in the rear of the craft, reading over

the latest data sent back by the drilling station. Jacob was a geologist specializing in alluvial sedimentation and had done field work on Europa. Before that he had served on Mars, working with Dr. Ravencroft on what became known as the Ravencroft Drilling Technique: a novel way of quickly extracting and analyzing soil samples. Jacob's discovery of underground rivers in the north polar region had established his name in scientific circles. It was hoped that Martian microbes inhabited the rivers, but none were ever discovered. He was in his early forties, divorced, with a son and daughter back on Earth.

"Think they'll find anything this time?" It was Martha. "Ravencroft seemed pretty excited."

"Doubt it," Ken replied. "Probably just another false alarm. How many have there been?"

"A couple dozen," Martha replied with a frown.

Eighteen drilling stations were in operation, seventeen in Shangri-La and one in Adiri (another half-dozen were planned for that region). Each robotic drill plumbed to a depth of one meter and retrieved six cubic centimeters of substrata. This was transferred to a suite of three machines: the mass spectrometer, the subsurface mass analyzer, and the gas chromatograph. A sample was examined, and the results transmitted to Base Alpha every two hours. Similar drilling stations had been in operation on Mars and Europa for years. The brainchild of Dr. Ravencroft, it revolutionized planetary exploration. The drilling stations had been in operation for over six months and had uncovered nothing but sludge.

Gamma-24, the sole drilling station in Adiri, lay sixty kilometers east of Base Alpha. It was situated near one of several ponds in the area. The sludge that had been extracted contained the usual assortment of minerals and organic material, but no signs of life. Yet *something* had triggered an alarm.

"I'd say," Jacob broke in, pulling himself away from a video screen, "that Ravencroft needs to rework his experiment. Develop equipment that can drill down a hundred meters. A single meter won't do. Seismic experiments indicate the substrata changes dramatically at the lower levels." He scratched the side of his nose and sniffed. "What do we have so far? We've discovered a tantalizing soup of organic compounds. But they could have been seeded by asteroid impacts or even ejecta from Saturn's rings. There's nothing definitive as far as life is concerned. Only one logical conclusion: we've got to probe deeper. Much deeper."

"Ravencroft doesn't think so," Ken said. "He's convinced conditions for life are amenable near the surface, at least for complex life forms, which, he says, is all NASA cares about. Anything less than their discovery would mean failure in his eyes."

"That's absurd," Martha said.

"Nevertheless, that's what he believes. If you ask me, he's been acting erratically lately. Perhaps the pressure is getting to him. Or maybe it's a result of the space out here." Ken meant it as a joke, but nobody laughed.

"Suit up," Jacob said. "We're almost there."

The Adiri Plateau was a hilly area with methane rivers that ran down to a central plain covered with pebbles. Its hills were composed mainly of dense water ice. They teemed with organic compounds which rained down from Titan's thick atmosphere. The rain-filled ponds—it was hoped—had sparked some form of life.

That was Dr. Ravencroft's theory, anyway.

They were approaching Gamma-24 when the storm hit. Visibility dropped to zero in a matter of seconds. They saw swirling colors of pink, red, and dark brown, heard particles raining down on the hovercraft. Even the craft's headlamps were unable to penetrate the thick methane fog. Autopilot took over and brought them in the rest of the way.

Titan's drilling stations, like those on Mars and Europa, were encased in pressurized bubbles. They protected the labs and provided life support for maintenance visits. When the hovercraft arrived, the storm had begun to subside, and the crew entered the station without incident.

But then, as is so often the case on Titan, the

weather proved to be mercurial once again. They removed their helmets just in time to hear a ferocious clap of thunder. Three more claps followed in quick succession, and a methane rain erupted from blackened skies. They gazed out a window at the scene before them. Streaks of lightning lit up the rock-strewn landscape. They saw a rain so thick it was like a red curtain descending. But because of Titan's thick atmosphere and low gravity, the raindrops fell at the speed snowflakes fall on Earth.

***

A low whistle. "Look at this!"

It was Martha, pointing at the sludge bucket.

Ken and Jacob were beside her in a flash, just in time to see six wormlike organisms slithering out of sight into the sludge.

To say they were shocked was an understatement. The area had been extensively analyzed and nothing indicated the existence of multicellular life, only the possibility of methane-based microbes.

Yet there it was. Life. Jacob took out a small metal rod from a tool case and tapped the sludge bucket. Nothing. He tapped the pebbles and subsoil. Again, nothing. He made a depression in the soil and stirred. A moment later one of the organisms emerged. It was thirty centimeters long, jet black. A second creature poked through. This one was the same length, but lighter in color.

Martha radioed Base Alpha. They were told to seal the bucket and return with it the next day, after the storm had passed.

***

"Where did they come from?" It was Fred Bouche, chief biologist. Fred was a short, heavyset man with a jaw like a block of granite. "Couldn't have been a drilling sample. The worms are too damn big."

"Gamma-24 is located at the edge of Blackwater Pond," Martha said. "Maybe they live in the pond?"

"Water samples show no evidence of life. No organic compounds. Nothing. Besides, if they came from the pond, how did they get into the sealed station?"

The scientists were in Base Alpha's main analysis lab, one of the largest rooms in the compound. It was packed with equipment: spectrometers, imagers, microscopes, computers, and several gene analyzers. Fred was hovering over an analyzer, feeding it data about the worms' structure.

"Give us a few hours and we'll know more," he said.

Ken strode into the room, carrying a tablet. "Take a look at this," he said, putting it down on a desk.

Martha glanced over his shoulder. "More worms," she sighed. "Taking pictures of our new friends?"

He shook his head. "Planaria."

"What?"

"Didn't you notice? The worms look like Earth planaria. Much larger, true, but the overall structure is the same. Slender bodies. Triangular heads with two eye spots. A central white striation running the length of the body."

"That would be quite a coincidence," Martha said with a touch of sarcasm.

"Right. It was simply an observation."

"An *interesting* observation." It was Fred Bouche, turning to face them. He rubbed his chin and added, "Planarians are among the earliest representatives of the phylum Platyhelminthes and have been around for millions of years." He looked over at one of the microscopes. "What do you think you get if you cut a planaria in two?"

"A dead planaria?" Ken chuckled.

"Two living planaria. Two *identical* living planaria. They are essentially immortal, being composed primarily of pluripotent stem cells. As such, they have existed virtually unchanged for all that time. They are nearly impossible to kill and have been found in every habitat on Earth, from the polar caps to the equator. It's possible they migrated from Earth after a period of meteoric bombardment. Of course, gene analysis will give us a conclusive answer."

***

When Martha walked into Fred's lab several hours later, he was staring at a computer screen with a nervous frown.

"Martha," Fred said, looking up from the screen. "Boy, am I glad to see you."

"That doesn't sound good."

"Those worms . . ."

"Titanian organisms, right?"

Fred groaned. "Hardly. Ken's planaria. Turns out they don't just *look* like Earth planaria. They *are* Earth planaria."

Martha gasped.

"I've run the data through the analyzer twice with the same results. Down to the last gene these creatures are identical to *Schmidtea mediterranea*, a species of planaria used in genomic research."

"That can't be. They're larger than common planaria, for one thing."

"That's what confused me. At first. They've been genetically altered to resemble an extraterrestrial species."

"You mean they were planted? How is that possible?"

Fred explained. "Normally, a genetically altered organism is easily detected by running its genomic structure through a gene analyzer and comparing it against a database of known gene sequences. Subtle variations from a known sequence are detected by the analyzer with near one hundred percent accuracy. The Optima database we use lists literally millions of sequences. And, in fact, the first time I ran our organism's sequence through the analyzer it found no variations from any known sequences, yet no matches either. In other words, it looked like a completely new organism. The *Schmidtea mediterranea* genome was related, true, but even so there were significant structural differences in the genetic code. But then I noticed something odd. One of the differences reported was the sequence GATTTAGCAA and the related sequence GAUUUABCAA, where uracil, a protein that replaces thymine in RNA, appears in the DNA sequence. RNA is responsible for the expression of genes, not the structure itself.

"So, when I programmed the analyzer to substitute uracil for thymine in those sequences, the Titan organism's genome was identified as a variant of *Schmidtea mediterranea*. In other words, whoever did this was able to convert some of the organisms' DNA into RNA and thus alter not the genes themselves, but the gene's *expression*. The result: larger than life but otherwise quite ordinary planaria. Mutants, basically. The work of Man."

Martha uttered a low whistle.

"I was lucky. If I hadn't run the data through the analyzer a second time, I never would have noticed the match. But I did. And that means someone else's luck has just run out."

"Who would have the knowledge to do this?"

Fred took a deep breath. "I would, of course. And I can think of several people on Earth." He bit his lip, his face reddening. "Oh, and there's one other person."

"Yes?"

"Dr. Ravencroft."

"Ravencroft? That's crazy, Fred. Surely you're not implying the man would rig his own experiment?"

"Why not? Maybe because it *is* his experiment. He's spent years on this mission. Having found nothing, he needs to give it the illusion of success. I'm sure you're aware of the latest reports from Earth. This is the most expensive mission in the history of the space program. There's talk of budgetary cuts. *Severe* cuts. Heck— there's talk of scrapping the entire mission!"

Martha shrugged. "I've been with NASA ten years. I can't recall a time when that *wasn't* the case."

"I'm afraid it might really be true this time."

"Besides," Martha said after a short pause, "aren't you jumping the gun? There's no proof Ravencroft did anything."

"None at all."

"What to do?"

"Nothing," Fred said, "but wait."

"And aren't you forgetting one other thing? The worms. What's to be done about *them*?"

"My report will show exactly what I've found. And we take it to Ravencroft. Honestly, Martha, I don't know who is behind this, but one thing I do know: those worms are no more native to this place than you or I."

***

"I see." It was Dr. Ravencroft. He was seated at his office desk, gazing at Martha and Fred who sat across from him, looking grim. "I see—but I don't understand. Who would do such a thing—and why? Surely they'd realize any such doctoring would eventually be discovered."

"Doesn't make sense to us, either," Martha said. "Unless . . ."

Dr. Ravencroft was stone-faced. "Unless what?"

"You can't deny that, until now, we've found nothing on Titan," Fred said, brusquely. "The pressure to produce positive results must be immense."

Dr. Ravencroft scowled. "If either of you believe I'd succumb to such pressure . . . I urge you to speak plainly!"

"No," Fred replied. "We don't believe it. But it does seem like a logical explanation. And that means NASA is likely to believe it. And that would spell the end of this mission and of the search for life on the outer worlds for some time to come."

"And we can't have that," Martha interjected. Her hazel eyes were burning brightly.

Dr. Ravencroft sighed. "I agree with you completely," he said. "And that's why we must keep this to ourselves." He eyed them closely. "Agreed?"

Martha looked at him uneasily. "Yes," she said. "That's the best course."

***

The official report, as relayed to Earth, said the warning on drilling station Gamma-24 was due to a computer malfunction: a cooling unit had begun to fail intermittently. The problem was corrected when a new unit was swapped in. There was no mention of organisms, extraterrestrial or otherwise. As far as NASA was concerned, the only thing found during six months of testing were traces of organic compounds. That wasn't what they wanted to hear, after literally thousands of soil samples had been analyzed, but it was preferable to learning that the entire experiment may have been rigged.

Nothing out of the ordinary happened for the next six weeks, at least as far as the search for life was concerned. There was, however, an incident involving several members of the team, including Dr. Ravencroft, that nearly ended in tragedy. It occurred when they were engaged in field work inside Crater Miranda, which was located on the southern edge of Shangri-La, about 150 kilometers from Base Alpha. The scientists were surveying the area, having flown out in a hovercraft earlier that morning.

The sky was salmon-pink and dotted with thick, gray clouds composed of methane and cyanide gas. The nearby terrain was smooth, but farther away there were narrow gullies, like furrows in a farmer's field. The team had encountered such depressions before; in fact, they were ubiquitous in the Shangri-La region. They were composed of frozen methane nodules and water ice mixed with sedimentary pebbles. It was believed that the gullies had been formed by rivers of methane which flowed across the plain, depositing the building blocks of life.

Titan's atmosphere was thick and its gravity low, resulting in a surface pressure only one-and-a-half times that of Earth. In fact, pressurized suits weren't needed to compensate for the moon's atmospheric pressure; instead, they offered protection from the cold and Titan's poisonous atmosphere. Because of the low illumination, surface features were obscured; it was as if one were looking at the landscape through fogged lenses of odd curvature. And now, as the scientists worked inside the crater with its rim rising around them, it all led to a surreal, claustrophobic feeling that was quite disorienting.

"Dr. Ravencroft. You okay?" It was Paul Mercer, a member of the biology team. He had noticed the chief scientist gazing about for what seemed an inordinately long time.

Just at that moment Dr. Ravencroft swooned and crumpled to the ground.

He was hurriedly brought back aboard the hovercraft. His helmet was removed, and oxygen administered. His face was ashen, but he quickly revived.

A hole the size of a pin was discovered in his spacesuit the next day back at Base Alpha. It might have been caused by high-velocity dust particles which were known to rain down during the occasional dust storm. The suits were checked before every excursion, but that didn't mean a breach might not go undetected.

Dr. Ravencroft was placed under observation in the medical wing for twenty-four hours. He complained once or twice of feeling light-headed and of an unsettled stomach. The medical technician said that was normal, the result of having succumbed to Titan's noxious gases, however briefly.

Even so, his stay was extended another twenty-four hours, just to be certain he was fully recovered. During that period, he was visited by everyone on Base Alpha, most notably Fred Bouche who spent hours at his side.

He felt responsible, Fred told the med tech when the man came through later to check up on the patient. Raul had been under immense pressure and Fred's report only made things worse. If the chief scientist hadn't been so preoccupied, perhaps he would have spotted the compromised spacesuit. As it was, the mission very nearly ended right then and there. Without Dr. Ravencroft's leadership, and with little to show after months of work, NASA would have had no choice but to bring back the remaining members of the expedition.

On the morning of the second day, however, Dr. Ravencroft was pronounced recovered and he was released.

***

Two days later, in the early morning hours, an alarm was triggered on drilling station Gamma-32 in the central Adiri plain.

Once again Martha, Ken, and Jacob suited up and boarded the hovercraft. The journey to Gamma-32 was uneventful. The light was dim as usual, not much brighter than Earth under a full moon, but it was that rarest of Titanian days when the clouds parted to reveal a dull red sky with streaks of pink and orange. The extra visibility allowed them to see the hills of Adiri in the distance. Titan's misty veil having lifted, giant Saturn loomed softly overhead, filling nearly a third of the sky. It was a spectacular sight.

At about the halfway point a call came in from Base Alpha. It was Jen Rogers in Communications. "Greetings, folks," she said cheerfully. "Looks like you're headed to the right place. Today's report from Gamma-32 just came in. Microbial life. It's been detected."

"On Gamma-32?" It was Martha.

"No doubt about it. According to the data, methane-based multicellular life forms. And something else, though we're not sure what."

Ken and Jacob whooped and hollered. Martha was more subdued. "Could be more of those fake worms," she said.

And that's what they found when they entered the airlock of Gamma-32, thirty minutes later. Hundreds of organisms slithering across the floor and climbing the walls, leaving green, sticky slime in their wake. They looked like the organisms on Gamma-24. But they were much larger. Up to a meter in length. And then there was that residue . . .

"These things weren't extracted during the drilling process," Martha said. "And they definitely aren't Earth planaria."

Jacob grimaced. "If someone's playing a trick on us, they have an odd sense of humor."

"This is no trick," Ken said. "These things are real. Some mutant life forms. Fred is going to want one to examine."

"How do you propose we—" Martha began, but stopped short when she heard a sound from an adjacent room. The main lab.

They entered cautiously, expecting to find more of the worms slithering about. There were none. They did see several sludge buckets, all empty, and, near the front of the room, a subsoil analyzer and two computer stations.

Unfortunately, that wasn't all they found.

A body. A human body, slumped over a computer terminal, about ten meters away. There was a fist-sized hole in the back of the spacesuit. Blasted with a laser gun. The fabric was blackened, and blood oozed from the wound.

Martha uttered a cry and rushed towards the body.

From the shadows in the back of the room, Fred Bouche emerged with his laser weapon drawn. Both Jacob and Ken saw the movement and wheeled around. Martha was fixated on the body and did not notice. Fred glared at Jacob and Ken with icy eyes, then trained his weapon on Martha.

Jacob cried out, "Bouche, put that weapon down!"

Hearing Jacob's words, Martha tumbled to the floor. Fred fired but missed, the laser beam hitting one of the drilling station's generators which exploded in a shower of sparks and debris.

"Game's up, Bouche," Jacob said. "We know what's going on between you and Ravencroft."

In response, Bouche aimed his weapon at the

opposite wall and fired. The beam hit the wall, which exploded, raining debris throughout the room and fracturing a section of an embedded window. How many more blasts could the structure take before Titan's poisonous atmosphere leaked in, overcoming them all?

"Don't be a fool," Jacob said.

Bouche laughed and pointed the gun at the window. "One more shot should do it," he said. His face was red with rage.

"Fred, good God, no!" Jacob cried. "Don't throw away your life like this."

A moment of hesitation from Bouche was just enough.

Taking advantage of the chaos, Ken had maneuvered off to the side and along the wall, and now he lunged forward, tackling Bouche and pinning him to the floor.

Bouche dropped the weapon and burst into tears.

"Got him!" Ken cried to Martha. She picked herself up off the floor and quickly reached the terminal, turned the body over and saw the turgid face of Dr. Raul Ravencroft, his features frozen in the agony of death. "Raul?" she said in disbelief. "Oh, my God . . ."

Jacob rushed over, saw the body, and recoiled in horror. "Perhaps not," he stammered. "Look at his eyes . . . no, not eyes. Eye-spots. Planarian ocelli."

Martha's own eyes opened wide in disbelief. There was a gaping hole in Ravencroft's chest, and the cavity was swarming with baby planaria. "What happened to him?" she gasped. "And his face . . ." She forced herself to look away.

"Jacob! Martha! Over here." It was Ken. "What in the world is this?"

Jacob slung the dead scientist's body over his shoulder. He and Martha made their way across the lab to where Ken was kneeling.

"Ravencroft's been murdered," Martha told the astonished technician. "Laser bolt through the chest."

Jacob pointed. "Bouche?"

"Or what's left of him," Ken replied. "Look at that . . ."

It was a planaria, clinging to the side of Fred Bouche's neck. Slimy, acidic, hypnotically undulating.

And in the scientist's countenance, there was an eerie alien expression. Probing. Questioning. And undoubtedly intelligent.

Martha screamed.

Another explosion. This time from outside the lab.

"Let's get out of here!" It was Jacob. "Life support's been breached. The whole place is on fire!"

They carried the limp body of Raul Ravencroft and a weeping Fred Bouche to the hovercraft. En route to Base Alpha, Martha radioed the news. "One dead," she told a startled Jen Rogers. "One . . . status unknown."

***

The alien organism had not attached itself to Bouche, as they had assumed. Rather, it had grown from within. The appendage was surgically removed and placed in a specimen dish for study. It certainly looked like a Titanian planaria. Only in miniature. About ten centimeters long, two centimeters wide. And covered in translucent greenish slime. A culture was taken and sent off to the lab for analysis.

But everyone knew what must have happened.

"Infected by the organisms he studied," said the doctor, Herbert Richter, when the results came back. "The only questions are where and when it occurred. And how it was able to infect the host body."

Answers that would need to come from Fred Bouche.

When Bouche recovered from surgery, he confessed to the planting of evidence and the murder of the Chief Mission Scientist.

"They made me do it," he said to Sally Gimble, acting Base Commander. Gimble was forty-six years old, a veteran of colonies on the moon and Mars. Well-respected. And wicked-smart.

"They?"

"The worms."

She eyed him closely. "Fred, how did you get infected?"

"Some type of alien osmosis, I guess." Bouche shrugged. "We followed proper lab procedures. Must be

~ 205 ~

something we don't understand." His voice was harsh and raspy. It was as if he was forcing out the words.

Gimble paused. There was no easy way to say this. "Tissue samples show planarian DNA throughout your system."

"Yes."

"Are they controlling you now?"

"I don't know. I think so. They must be."

"Why do you say that?"

"Because I feel like I'm underwater. In some deep, dark Titanian lake."

Richter broke in, "He's fighting something, Sally. I don't know how much of this we can trust—if anything."

"Fred—" Her tone was sharp.

"Yes?"

"What did they have you do?"

His reply was immediate. And insistent. "They made me sabotage the DNA Analyzer results. And then announce I'd discovered the altered data. They want our mission to fail. They want us to leave." Bouche sighed. "There was no malfeasance. On my part. Or Ravencroft's."

"Why not simply attack us?"

"Better to lead us to believe there was no life on Titan. Then we would move on. Isn't that what you would have done?"

Gimble turned to Richter and said, "Whether it's intelligence or not is open to question, but it does make sense. In a twisted sort of way."

"When Ravencroft discovered what I had done, he followed me out to Gamma-32," Bouche continued. "He confronted me. Wanted to know what the hell I thought I was doing. He'd been infected, too, but not to the degree I had. Not yet, anyway. I don't think he realized, yet, what was happening. It was only a matter of time, though, and then . . ." His voice trailed off.

Moments later he was fast asleep.

***

"Ever hear of epigenetics?" Jacob asked of a bewildered Ken and Martha the next evening as they were discussing events in the base lounge.

Neither responded readily.

"The modification of the genetic make-up of a species," Jacob continued. "Bouche was right about the altered planarian structure, but wrong about what caused it. On Earth, epigenetic factors cause slight alterations in the expression of the genetic code. On Titan, apparently their effect is greatly magnified. We're dealing with alien life forms far more advanced than what anyone thought we'd encounter."

Martha nodded. "So, it's akin to the old nature/nurture controversy of the twentieth-century?"

"Updated for the twenty-first century. Epigenetic factors don't change the DNA structure, they change how the structure is read: the *epigenome*. And it's more complex than DNA. A gene sequence is basically fixed throughout life; epigenetic markers differ in tissue types and vary over time."

"Possibly a result of environmental factors," Ken interjected. "Which explains . . ."

"Precisely. Think of the epi as software, the DNA as hardware. Titanian planaria have the same DNA sequence as the Earth variety, but, because of vastly different environmental conditions, the expression of the sequence is far different. It's still odd, though—how the exact same genetic structure could evolve across the span of space."

"It's something we can never really predict or account for," Martha said. She took a deep breath. "I wonder if Raul knew what was happening to him? The horror he must have felt."

"We're left with a problem," Ken said a moment later. "What happens to Bouche? We're a billion kilometers from Earth. Our medical facilities weren't setup to handle anything like this. And we certainly can't risk letting the infection spread."

Jacob frowned. "Nothing we can do. Bouche must be kept in isolation. We can only assume that the planaria will slowly destroy him—or drive him mad—but maybe not. With life as strange as this, who knows what might happen next." He turned slowly from Martha to Ken, saw worry etched in their faces. "Look. Bouche knew the risks of this mission like the rest of us. If anyone can pull him through this, though, it's Richter."

They nodded grimly.

Sadly, it was not to be. Fred Bouche died two weeks later, writhing in agony, a mass of pulpy planarian flesh. The isolation chamber was promptly irradiated, destroying any alien organisms that remained.

The mood on Base Alpha was somber, as it was back at NASA when news of Fred's death was received. With the loss of two top scientists, a shadow had been cast over the entire mission. A review of the mission was undertaken back on Earth, as protocol demanded, but which was unsettling to the research team nevertheless, and when word came back from NASA, it was met with sighs of relief: There would be no letup. The work must go on.

"Who would have imagined one of the most ancient Earth species would be waiting to greet mankind in the far reaches of the solar system?" Jacob posed to Ken and Martha shortly thereafter. They were hard at work in Base Alpha's main lab, Jacob firing up the DNA analyzer to examine samples Ken had just brought in from Gamma-16.

Martha nodded. "A sobering thought."

PUFF

66 Good God." George Trevor pulled himself away from the computer screen, his light-brown eyes opened wide in disbelief. He was in Professor Crews' Exoplanetary Research Lab on Stanford University's main campus.

He swept a hand through thick, dark hair. "It's the signature we've been looking for, Nance. I can't believe it."

Nancy Simmons was on the other side of the lab, filing this week's data sets from the high-resolution interferometer. The professor had an inherent distrust in computers and made his assistants file hard copies of all lab results.

She spun around. "What did you find?"

George took a deep breath. "Exactly as we hypothesized, Nance. Pulses of energy at the M32 and C5 bands."

The two lab assistants had spent the last year scanning the constellation Cygnus looking for signs of extraterrestrial life. It was a project made possible by the launch of BioProbe, a satellite whose mission was to identify exoplanets and analyze their atmospheres, searching for unusual spectra or energy bursts which might indicate the presence of life.

"Let's have a look!" It was Professor Crews, striding into the lab wearing his wrinkled white lab coat. The professor was a giant of a man with bushy jet-black hair, luminous dark eyes, and a prominent goatee. In his right hand he held a stack of scientific journals. He set them on the table, then crossed the room to examine George's computer screen.

"Quite a match," he said, as he stroked his beard. "Isn't that planet X35 in the Sigma system?"

Identified early-on as an Earth-like world, X35 had been closely monitored by the lab for some time.

"No, it's X37," George replied. X37 was at the outer edge of the system's habitable zone. It was twice the size of Earth, possessed only a tenuous atmosphere, and had garnered far less attention.

Nancy broke in. "The data we've been examining is six months old. It was obtained when we were performing a scan of the Sigma system. Our initial analysis turned up nothing, that is, no anomalies were observed at the frequencies we were monitoring. It turns out we were looking for the wrong thing. We'd assumed that an abnormal increase in oxygen, methane, or carbon dioxide levels in a planet's atmosphere would indicate the presence of life. Now, that's a plausible assumption, so we can't be blamed for thinking it was the case."

"But it wasn't," George interjected, rising from a stool so the professor could take a closer look. "Turns out the evidence was on another band, one that showed signs of chemical activity on the planet's surface. The activity was metabolic in nature. If anabolism is detected it almost certainly means—"

"Life." Professor Crews pulled himself away from the computer screen. "In all probability, highly evolved life. On X37."

"Let's not jump to conclusions," George said. "Life,

yes. But highly evolved?"

Dr. Crews was adamant. "The chemical signature mirrors exactly what extraterrestrials would observe of Earth! We must, therefore, assume the existence of a technological civilization. Most likely on the order of our own. I am confident that further results will substantiate my hypothesis."

All other possibilities were eventually ruled out, and on the twenty-fourth of March 2073, the results were published in the *Journal of Intragalactic Exploration.*

***

Nuclear fission is the splitting apart of atomic nuclei. The process was perfected in the mid-twentieth century. It was the basis of the world's nuclear industry by 2050, accounting for forty percent of the world's energy needs. Unfortunately, nuclear fission was a political nightmare. No one wanted radioactive byproducts in their backyard.

Everyone realized that nuclear *fusion*—the energy source which powered the stars—was the ultimate answer. But the technology was complex and expensive, with half-a-dozen theoretical problems still to be worked out, most important of which was how to bottle up the high-temperature gases needed to make fusion feasible.

That is, until now.

"Gentleman, I believe we have a breakthrough." Professor Fred Gable's dark-brown eyes sparkled as he slammed his fist down on the lab bench in triumph. "Yes!"

The Caltech Thermonuclear Research Laboratory was a twelve-person lab composed of physicists, materials engineers, and graduate students. Under the direction of Professor Gable, the lab had been working for years on what was termed the thermonuclear plasma containment problem.

The lab's first attempts were met with failure. In traditional reactor technology, magnetic fields were used to confine and control plasma flow through the reactor. A large current was induced by changing the direction of the magnetic field. The current flowed perpendicular to the field and heated the plasma to the enormous temperatures required. At that point, plasma flowed freely along magnetic field lines.

The lab found that heating plasma to one hundred million kelvins wasn't the issue; it was the inability to control plasma flow once stellar temperatures were reached. Magnetic field generation was the key, but the mathematical problems were complex. A new set of algorithms needed to be developed, and work towards that end had been painfully slow.

But all of that was behind them.

"Three cheers for Professor Gable!" The chant echoed throughout the lab. A bottle of champagne was uncorked. No doubt about it, everyone knew who was tops in the running for this year's Nobel Prize in Physics.

The breakthrough was announced on June 18, 2073. Professor Gable said that a prototype reactor was at most two years away, with the first commercial reactor available within a decade. A limitless supply of pollution-free energy would be at hand.

***

Dr. Herbert Sloan, Director of Planetary Missions at NASA's Langley Research Center in Hampton, Virginia, was gazing out the window of his office on the eighth floor of the agency's administration building. He'd been going over plans for a proposed mission to Titan, recently sent over from the agency's Science Mission Directorate. It sounded interesting. Damn interesting. The Cassandra mission to Saturn had sent a probe beneath Titan's surface, confirming that the moon's methane lakes extended for kilometers. More astonishingly, the probe found evidence of lakes composed of liquid water. And that meant there was a good chance life existed there as well. The Huygens II Mission, scheduled to launch in early 2075, would send a probe loaded with advanced scientific instruments to determine if life did in fact exist.

Dr. Sloan's cell phone rang.

"Sloan here."

It was Jordan Roberts, one of Langley's top geological engineers. "Just got off the phone with Professor Crews over at Stanford," he said excitedly. "The old man wanted to know what I knew about exoplanet geology. I told him there wasn't any such discipline. Crews said, 'There will be soon.'"

"They find something?" Dr. Sloan knew about Dr. Crews' project to detect the conditions for life on exoplanets. He'd even agreed to Crews' request to point BioProbe at the Sigma system for an extended period, when it meant bumping other—more vocal—research groups. And initial results had *not* been promising. Sloan took heat for that.

"Forget about biomarkers," Roberts said. "Dr. Crews claims they've found evidence of an advanced civilization on X37." He let the words sink in. "And from what I see of the preliminary data, he might be right."

"I'll be right over." Dr. Sloan hung up, told his secretary he'd be in engineering the rest of the afternoon. As for the mission to Titan, it would have to wait.

***

The news was met with stunned disbelief. That extraterrestrial civilizations existed—or had existed in the past—was considered likely. But this was cold, hard evidence. Chemical and biological markers that could not be denied. And the exoplanet was close at hand: the Sigma star system was only four light-years from Earth.

Earth faced a dilemma. Should it attempt to contact the planet? A meeting of the United Nations was held July 21 at which numerous proposals were put forward. Arguments were presented for both sides.

With no consensus—and apparently none possible— NASA made the unilateral decision to send a message to X37. Traveling at the speed of light, it would be a four-year journey. Even if a civilization recognized it as an alien greeting, it would be another four years for any reply.

"You know what this means?" Professor Crews said to George and Nancy when news of NASA's space message was announced. "Nothing less than an evolution in human consciousness. Why, in the near future we may find ourselves living in a society as far advanced over our modern-age as it is above the Paleolithic!"

Nancy frowned. "Provided we're not eaten by marauding aliens."

"I don't know about that," George laughed.

In the months that followed, Dr. Crews' lab continued crunching data. And numbers kept pouring in from BioProbe. A follow-up mission was scheduled for March 2075: BioProbe 2.

***

"This can't be." Professor Harvey Wasserman, head investigator of the Planetary Research Laboratory, Imperial College, London, wiped a hand across his sweaty brow. He was a tall, thin man with lively blue eyes. An expert in his field and well-respected. "There's nothing there. Nothing at all."

The lab had made a startling discovery. Utilizing the same methods as the Stanford lab, but analyzing data from a different sector of the galaxy, they found no indication of life, advanced or primitive.

"Statistically speaking there should be *some* signal to find," said astrobiologist Marge Lewinsky. She'd been at the Stanford lab when the initial discovery was announced. "It doesn't invalidate what Crews detected. But it calls into question his theory of how life propagates through a galactic system."

According to Dr. Crews, since physical laws were the same everywhere, it made sense that when planetary conditions were suitable evolutionary forces would ensure life developed. Surveys found that planetary systems were evenly distributed throughout the galaxy. And that meant life should be evenly distributed throughout the galaxy as well.

"That could still be true," Lewinsky continued. "But

maybe its distribution is on a larger scale than we envisioned."

"You mean life is rarer than we thought."

"Yes."

Professor Wasserman nervously drummed a lab desk. "Perhaps. Or it could mean . . ."

There had always been skeptics, those who wondered if Dr. Crews had erred in the analysis of the original data. After all, his methods were novel and complex. Since extraterrestrial biology might well depend on different chemical processes, might there be another explanation? BioProbe 2 would put an end to all speculation. But it would be months before results from the probe would become available. The scientific community would simply have to wait.

***

Visiting Professor Jennifer Piorka was in Stanford's astrophysics lab the day data from BioProbe 2 began to arrive. Though not a member of the team examining X37's data, Dr. Piorka had followed the investigation with interest. She was from the Max Planck Institute for Physics in Munich and had been at Stanford the past year. Ambitious and beautiful, she was often found poking about in the labs, to the delight of the male staff.

One day she broached the possibility to Professor Crews that an extraterrestrial civilization's fusion reactors might be detectable.

"A molecular effusion cloud, produced by such a reactor, would make detection relatively straightforward," she said.

He seemed intrigued. "And the defining means . . .?"

"Hydrogen and tritium transition radio lines. No natural process could account for their presence."

"Yes."

"The problem is that the cloud rapidly disassociates to a ground atomic state."

"In other words, detection must be quick."

"Within days."

Professor Crews nodded. "If current research comes to a dead end, that may be our next area of investigation!"

***

It was November 14, 2075, a day that would be remembered throughout human history. It was the day mankind fired up the world's first nuclear-powered fusion reactor. The Gabletron, as it was known at Caltech, heated plasma to a temperature of one-hundred million kelvins, though only for a tenth of a second and in micro quantities. It was merely proof of concept, but that was all it was intended to be.

"We've reached the throne of the gods!" Professor Gable intoned when the critical plasma temperature was reached.

Now came the hard part: securing funding for a full-scale reactor. After an intense year-long campaign, a billion dollars was pledged, and an engineering and construction team was put together. The total number of scientists involved was nearly three hundred and was expected to double by the time the project was in full swing.

Ground was broken near Austin, Texas in the spring of 2076. Gabletron II. It would be a massive five-year effort: a two-hundred-meter-wide ring of gleaming metal, with thousands of magnetic coils surrounding the ring and generating the magnetic fields which induced current in the plasma.

The ring was completed on schedule and within budget after eighteen months. Next up: the magnetic coils. Because of Dr. Gable's design breakthrough, this most difficult part of construction was greatly simplified. Two years later the coils were in place. Testing could commence.

During Test Phase 1, the ring was filled with helium, a non-reactive gas. The purpose of this phase was to make certain the gas could be heated, and plasma flow controlled. Two months later, Test Phase 2. The helium was replaced with tritium, an isotope of hydrogen. When heated to a temperature five times that of the sun, the isotope became a plasma, an ionized gas consisting of free electrons and unbound nuclei. Fusion occurred when these nuclei were forced together. And that was the job of the current induced by the magnetic field.

It was a gradual process, slowly increasing the reactor's capacity until the necessary temperature was attained.

"All systems go," Professor Gable declared.

***

Dr. Crews' next directive was to expand the lab's research to included unexamined regions of the sky. That required a proposal to convince NASA to give the lab more time with BioProbe 2. After the usual lobbying effort, a proposal was accepted and extra time apportioned. The lab could not have been more pleased when data came streaming in. Over a period of eight months, they detected signs of three civilizations over a broad portion of the heavens. The technique, developed at Imperial College the year before, used Piontka-Wasserman algorithms to detect planetary fusion reactions.

"It's unbelievable," George said to Nancy as the two pored over data showing signs of life on a planet in the Tau Ceti system. "Tau b: strong tritium transition lines at fifteen hundred sixteen megahertz."

At the inner edge of its sun's habitable zone, the exoplanet was one of five that orbited Tau Ceti, a G-class star about twelve light-years from Earth.

Unfortunately, there was a problem. And it was a significant one. In the fall of 2080, not only did X37's signals vanish, but of the three-dozen known planetary signals, only eight were still detectable. The others had simply disappeared. Moreover, it was eight years since NASA's message to X37 and no reply had been received.

The mood in the lab was somber. Crazy theories reverberated throughout the popular press: There had never been signals. It was all a ruse, the real mission being to further weapons development. It was even alleged that Stanford's lab was in the government's pocket!

Dr. Crews rolled his eyes in dismay. "The signals were real," he said to George one afternoon. "And they were spread all over the sky."

George stroked his chin. "Perhaps we were in error . . ."

"And if our interpretation was correct?"

"Then something happened to the civilizations on those planets."

"Or they learned to mask their energy output. Or they moved on to another form of energy we're not able to detect. There could be any number of reasons!"

"I suppose so," George sighed. "Still, it seems to be happening with frightening regularity."

Exactly what scared George remained unspoken, but Dr. Crews thought he knew what it was.

***

Gabletron II reached full capacity on February 16, 2081. Three hundred million watts of fusion-powered energy. Enough to power a small city. But Professor Gable would not stop there. After delivering a series of lectures in America and abroad, he announced plans to form an international consortium to oversee construction of half-a-dozen mega-reactors spread over the globe, and, eventually, thousands of smaller units extending from those central hubs like spokes on a wheel, each powering a city or rural area. It would usher in a new era of an endless supply of clean, affordable energy.

In October 2081 Dr. Gable received the Nobel Prize in physics for his work on fusion reactor technology. In his acceptance speech, he said:

". . . as a civilization progresses, its energy requirements increase; at the same time the amount of energy the civilization can produce is bound by the limits of its technology. A point is reached at which the amount of energy which can be produced no longer equals or exceeds that which is required. The civilization must acquire the technology needed to produce its energy requirements—or it will stagnate and, eventually, die.

Though we have managed to survive the leap to primitive fusion technology, it, too, has limits. Eventually, we will need to evolve to the next level: harnessing the entire power output of a star. We must ask ourselves: will our race be able to meet that challenge when the moment is upon us?"

***

Dr. Crews was grim. The lab's research was going nowhere. Now *all* the signals had vanished. Moreover, in the past three months nothing new had been discovered. He had hoped it would come down to instrumentation failure, but tests indicated all systems were functioning normally. There must be another explanation. Unfortunately, the government was in no mood to commit funds to a third BioProbe mission. All anyone wanted to talk about was nuclear fusion. The fire of the Gods.

"The fire of the Gods," Dr. Crews said forlornly to George and Nancy when they brought the latest—negative—search results to his office. "What is man? A modern-day Prometheus thieving fire from Mount Olympus?"

Their attention was diverted by the latest announcement from Herb Slotsky, noted science writer for the *Los Angeles Times*, as it flashed across Professor Crews' computer screen.

". . . it will be a twenty-year project funded by the world's major powers. Twelve thousand fusion reactors. A massive ten-gigawatt grid. The greatest construction project the world has ever known. The mighty Gabletron III. A new era dawning for the human race!"

"The fire of the Gods," Dr. Crews repeated. "And when we ascend that mighty throne, will we have acquired the wisdom to wisely use the inferno we would then possess?" He glanced at the lab results before him. "Or will it be like that?"

***

"Nothing like it has been undertaken in the history of the Antarean race," Tec Sdinq, distinguished council head, emoted.

The Antareans, an ancient civilization in a far-flung section of the Milky Way, was embarking upon the first— *their* first—survey of galactic civilizations. They had spent the last ten thousand solar years colonizing their celestial neighborhood and had established colonies on hundreds of planets. But now they wished to expand their galactic presence into the rest of the galaxy—and that required knowing what other civilizations might be out there.

The Great Galactic Survey was begun in the year 12,605 and was estimated to take twenty-four Antarean solar years. Sdinq announced the council's intentions at the "Sixty-Sixth International Congress on Scientific Matters."

After explaining the survey's rationale and methodology, he concluded, "We hope the survey will confirm that we are the most advanced civilization inhabiting our galaxy (we have no wish to face a competing species) and expose promising civilizations which we can then plunder."

***

One day, while making an inventory of the galaxy's Orion Spur, Earth's celestial neighborhood, the Antareans observed the civilization on the third planet from its sun vaporize itself in a puff of radioactive debris caused by a massive thermonuclear explosion.

"And then it was heard from no more," one of the Antareans emoted. "Such a pity."

Its companion nodded.

The event was catalogued, without comment. And the Antareans moved on.

ABOUT THE AUTHOR

Brian Biswas

Brian Biswas has published dozens of stories in the United States as well as internationally. He writes in a literary style reminiscent of magical realism which attempts to convey a slightly exaggerated but internally consistent sense of reality. He also writes gothic or neo-gothic tales, and straightforward horror and science fiction stories, often tinged with fantastic elements.

Brian was born in Columbus, Ohio. He received a

B.A. in Philosophy from Antioch College in Yellow Springs, Ohio, and an M.S. in Computer Science from the University of Illinois at Urbana-Champaign. He lives in an old neighborhood in Chapel Hill, North Carolina with his wife, Elizabeth, and an ever-changing assortment of animals.

Books from Lillicat Publishers

Visions Anthology Series
Visions: Leaving Earth
Visions II: Moons of Saturn
Visions III: Inside the Kuiper Belt
Visions IV: Space Between Stars
Visions V: Milky Way
Visions VI: Galaxies
Visions VII: Universe (Rogue Star Press)

Northern Futures
TreeVolution
The Future Is Short: Science Fiction in a Flash
The Future Is Short, Volume 3: Science Fiction in a Flash
Dance With Me: My Journey Through Cancer
Sunshine & Shadow: Memories from a Long Life

ROGUE STAR PRESS
The Helena Orbit

DAWN LIGHT PRESS
The Night Blooming Jasmine in Your Heart

ALTERNATE UNIVERSE PRESS
Snake in the Grass

CROSSWORD PUZZLES
Great Quotes

VISIONS VII

UNIVERSE

EDITED BY CARROL FIX

VISIONS VI: *GALAXIES*

VISIONS VI

GALAXIES

EDITED BY CARROL FIX

VISIONS V
MILKY WAY

EDITED BY CARROL FIX

VISIONS II: MOONS OF SATURN

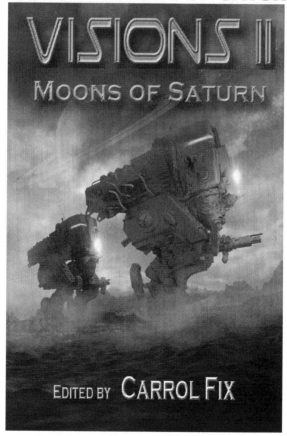

VISIONS: LEAVING EARTH